What if Striker didn't leave? What if the Marine Corps ordered him to stay?

She closed her eyes for a moment, imagining what it would be like…having him in her life permanently. Having this traveling marine settle down, marry, have kids. All with her.

"Do you want more?" Striker asked.

Her eyes flew open. "More?" Her voice was husky. No, she wouldn't want more than that. Having him safe by her side would be a dream come true.

But dreams didn't come true. Not for her.

Dear Reader,

Spring is here. And what better way to enjoy nature's renewed vigor than with an afternoon on the porch swing, lost in four brand-new stories of love everlasting from Silhouette Romance?

New York Times bestselling author Diana Palmer leads our lineup this month with *Cattleman's Pride* (#1718), the latest in her LONG, TALL TEXANS miniseries. Get to know the stubborn, seductive rancher and the shy innocent woman who yearns for him. Will her love be enough to corral his heart?

When a single, soon-to-be mom hires a matchmaker to find her a practical husband, she makes it clear she doesn't want a man who inspires reckless passion...but then she meets her new boss! In Myrna Mackenzie's miniseries THE BRIDES OF RED ROSE classic legends take on a whole new interpretation. Don't miss *Midas's Bride* (#1719)!

Her Millionaire Marine (#1720), from *USA TODAY* bestselling author Cathie Linz, and part of her MEN OF HONOR miniseries, finds a beautiful lawyer making sure the marine she secretly adores fulfills his grandfather's will. Falling in love with the daredevil is *not* part of the plan!

And Judith McWilliams's *Dr. Charming* (#1721) puts a stranded female traveler in the path of a mysterious doctor; she agrees to take a job in exchange for a temporary home—with him. Now, this man makes her want to explore passion, but can he tempt her to take the *ultimate* risk?

Sincerely,

Mavis C. Allen
Associate Senior Editor

Please address questions and book requests to:
Silhouette Reader Service
U.S.: 3010 Walden Ave., P.O. Box 1325, Buffalo, NY 14269
Canadian: P.O. Box 609, Fort Erie, Ont. L2A 5X3

Her
Millionaire
Marine

CATHIE LINZ

SILHOUETTE *Romance*®

Published by Silhouette Books

America's Publisher of Contemporary Romance

This book is dedicated to "AdCappy" Sarah Galanter, an extraordinary woman who loved romances and loved life. She was one in a million. She's greatly missed and will not be forgotten by those of us in her "crew."

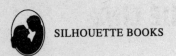 SILHOUETTE BOOKS

ISBN 0-373-19720-9

HER MILLIONAIRE MARINE

Copyright © 2004 by Cathie L. Baumgardner

Visit Silhouette Books at www.eHarlequin.com

Printed in U.S.A.

CATHIE LINZ

left her career in a university law library to become a *USA TODAY* bestselling author of contemporary romances. She is the recipient of the highly coveted Storyteller of the Year Award given by *Romantic Times* and was recently nominated for a Love and Laughter Career Achievement Award for the delightful humor in her books.

Although Cathie loves to travel, she is always glad to get back home to her family, her various cats, her trusty computer and her hidden cache of Oreo cookies!

Chapter One

Striker Kozlowski was a dead man. He knew it the instant he saw the top brass gathered in his C.O.'s office at the Marine Corps headquarters in Quantico, Virginia. His buddy Justice Wilder had warned him that one day he'd have to answer for his hotshot ways. Apparently today was that day.

None of Striker's thoughts showed as he saluted and stood at attention.

"At ease," Commander Jenks said. "As you know, this is a delicate situation, and while I can understand your reluctance to proceed, the bottom line is that there's only one thing to be done here."

"Agreed, sir," Striker said. "I'll apologize to the naval officer."

"What naval officer?"

So this wasn't about his fight with a naval officer in a bar last night? "Nothing, sir."

"As I was saying, we're all aware that you and your grandfather weren't close. He made no bones about the fact that he didn't approve of you being a Marine and he informed every senator and every general he met of that fact. I speak for us all when I say you have our condolences.''

"Thank you, sir." Condolences because he and his grandfather hadn't gotten along for years, or because the old man had never approved of Striker joining the Marine Corps instead of his oil company?

"His sudden death must still be dealt with," Commander Jenks added.

Striker went cold. His grandfather was dead? Not possible. Not Hank King, the mega-millionaire Texas oilman who was tougher than the walls of the Alamo and more stubborn than a packload of mules. Gone. Striker had a hard time wrapping his mind around that concept.

Somehow he'd always thought there would be time to sort things out, to mend the fences that had been broken when Striker had followed in his father's footsteps instead of falling into line by joining his maternal grandfather's oil business.

Striker had been trained well by the Marines, so his expression remained impassive as his emotions shut down and he went on autopilot.

The office door opened. "Ms. Kate Bradley, sir," the gunnery sergeant announced.

A female civilian rushed into the room on a cloud of expensive perfume. "I'm sorry I'm late, gentlemen," she said.

Striker recognized her type immediately. She was a ritzy blonde with high cheekbones and an elegant way about her. Her silky hair was drawn away from her face into some kind of intricate knot. The business suit she wore only hinted at the lush body beneath it. He was no expert on women's footwear, but he was willing to bet that the shoes she wore were Italian and probably cost more than he made in a month.

She radiated class. She also radiated sex appeal. And she was looking at him with disapproval even though he had yet to say a word. "I've been trying to get in touch with you since yesterday," Kate said, her cultured voice running over him like silk, "but you didn't return my calls."

"I apologize, ma'am." He said the words but he didn't mean them. "You never said what your call was in regard to."

"I assumed you'd already told Striker about his grandfather's passing," Commander Jenks said, clearly not pleased at this glitch in the game plan and holding Kate responsible for that fact.

She didn't even squirm, holding her ground as only those born and bred to wealth can. "As I said, I wasn't able to reach him."

"Let's cut to the bottom line here," Commander Jenks said. "Striker, your grandfather left an unusual codicil in his will regarding you."

"Sir, my grandfather disowned me years ago," Striker said.

"No, he didn't," Kate said. "He may have talked about doing that, but it was all bluster." Dropping onto a chair, she balanced her slim leather briefcase on her lap before opening it and removing a sheaf of papers. "I've come here today as his attorney and the executor of his will. His wish is that you come to Texas and run King Oil for a period of not less than two months."

"That dog's just not gonna hunt," Striker said, deliberately using a Texas phrase. "I'm a Marine, ma'am, not an oilman. I haven't had any contact with Hank King since I was nineteen and joined the Marines. That's been twelve years now. And even before that, we never had much of a relationship given the fact that he never approved of his only child, my mother, marrying a penniless nobody Marine named Kozlowski.''

''I tried to reach your mother to give her the news, but there was no answer at the number I had for her.''

''My parents are taking an extended vacation in a rented RV out west,'' Striker replied. ''I'll contact them on their cell phone right after this meeting.''

''I'm sorry for your loss,'' Kate said softly. ''If it makes it any easier for you, Hank died in his sleep. He wasn't in any pain.''

''As I said, I barely knew the man.'' Striker's voice was remote.

''Be that as it may, the terms of the will are very clear. You are to return to Texas with me and run King Oil for two months.''

Even saying the words ''return to Texas'' made Kate's stomach feel fluttery. She was trying to stay calm, but this meeting was much harder than she'd anticipated. When she'd walked into the office on the Marine base and realized that his commanding officer had broken the news to Striker, she'd felt both guilt and relief.

Not that Striker looked upset or emotional. He looked incredible but tough. The last time she'd seen him had been the last time he'd visited Hank. Striker had always been good-looking with his dark hair and green eyes, but the nineteen-year-old boy had grown into a combat-hardened man. There were lines on his face and shadows in his eyes that only hinted at the hardships he'd seen.

He obviously didn't remember meeting her that summer he'd worked on his grandfather's ranch so many years ago. But she remembered him. He'd played a pivotal part in her life, even though they'd barely met.

Closing her eyes, she was transported back in time to that fateful summer, when she was seventeen and had often ridden her Arabian horse Midnight over to the spring-fed pond that bordered their ranch with Hank's. The first time she'd seen Striker, he'd been stark naked, skinny-dipping in the cool waters on a sultry day. She could still see the droplets of water running down his muscular, tanned body. She'd silently watched him walk into the water, without making her presence known.

Not the proper behavior for a well-bred girl like herself. Especially given the fact that she was going steady with Ted at the time, and would become engaged to him a few months later, on her eighteenth birthday.

Kate's sexual fantasies about Striker had started then, and had only continued to increase that steamy summer. She'd seen Striker several other times, often finding him tossing hay in the barn wearing only well-washed jeans and a sheen of sweat.

Her mouth went dry at the memory....

Oh, yes, Striker had made a huge impression on her fanciful mind.

And now here she was, expected to return to Texas with him.

What on earth had made Hank think that she'd be able to deal with Striker? She'd tried to tell the oil baron that this was a bad idea, but he hadn't listened to her. The men in her life never seemed to listen to her. Not really.

"I'm thinking of going into public law," she'd told her father in her last year of law school.

"Nonsense. You'll join the family firm like we planned. You're a Bradley, and Bradleys always do as expected."

And so, in the end, she had. She'd done what was expected, including getting engaged to Ted Wentworth...with fatal results.

Kate took a soothing breath, before reminding herself that this was no time to be reviewing her life choices.

She had to keep her focus here. She had a feeling she'd need her wits about her in order to deal with Striker.

She knew he was a Force Recon Marine, which meant he was a risk taker. An adrenaline junkie, like Ted.

Opponents who faced her in court called her Ice Queen because of her regal demeanor and distant manner. She used those tactics now, opening her eyes and facing Striker. "As I said, your grandfather's will states that you return and run King Oil for at least two months or else the entire company will be shut down. If you do return with me, the King fortune will be split equally among you and your four brothers. In addition, a sizable amount will be bestowed upon your mother."

Striker told himself he shouldn't have been surprised that, even in his death, Hank King was trying to force him into this idiotic plan.

But Striker still held the ace in the hole. Money had never been important to his family. They'd managed okay without much of it. His mother believed that wealth had been a terrible burden and made Hank a bitter man.

"So King Oil is sold off," Striker said. "So what?"

"Perhaps I wasn't clear," Kate replied. "Everyone who works for King Oil will be out on the streets if you don't come back."

As if on cue, the Marine Corps' top brass, present but silent until now, explained their presence. General Hyett was their spokesman. "Top government officials are of the opinion that King Oil is too important to go under, that such a thing would make the economy unstable after the series of recent corporate bankruptcies. Therefore, it's in the country's best interest that Captain Kozlowski spend the two months at King Oil."

Striker had been trained to fight and rescue, to do whatever was necessary for his country's best interest.

No doubt his grandfather had counted on that when devising his will.

"Sir, I feel compelled to point out that I know nothing whatsoever about the oil business or about business in general," Striker said.

"That doesn't matter," General Hyett replied. "All you have to do is show up and stand guard for two months, then you can return to your regular duties. Isn't that right, ma'am? You said that would meet the terms of the will."

"That's right."

"Good. Then it's agreed," the general stated. "Look on this as just another mission, Captain. I'm sure you'll complete it as successfully as you have all the others."

Striker nodded curtly. He knew when he was beaten. "Thank you, sir."

"You and Ms. Bradley may use the conference room next door to work out the details," Commander Jenks told Striker. "That will be all. Dismissed."

Striker saluted before doing a precise about-face and heading for the door, which he held open for Kate. It wasn't until they were alone in the conference room that he displayed some of his pent-up frustration and anger.

"You and Hank had this all worked out, didn't you?" he growled.

"For your information, I told Hank that this wasn't a good idea," Kate replied in that highfalutin voice of hers.

"Bravo for you."

"He didn't listen to me."

"That's a pity."

"Look, I'm no happier about this state of affairs than you are."

"And why is that?"

"I've got better things to do with my time than deal

with stubborn Marines who have a chip on their shoulder.''

The woman clearly had an attitude problem. He knew why *he* was upset—he felt like his grandfather was still trying to control him even from beyond the grave. In addition, Striker had never done well dealing with the world of the rich and privileged.

He had his reasons, going all the way back to his time on Hank's Westwind Ranch. That had been his mom's idea. Hank had convinced her during one of their rare phone conversations that ''the boys'' should have a choice, should see what they were missing. Hank could have suggested having them work the rigs out in the oil fields, but instead he'd been wily enough to suggest they visit the ranch.

Striker wondered if his mom had ever been afraid her sons might be wooed over to the dark side by the wealth and the power visible at Westwind. Or if she'd trusted them to stand by the ethics and values she'd instilled in them from birth.

Sure, money had been tight when he'd been growing up. But there had never been a lack of respect, love or laughter in their household.

The same could not be said about the domain of Hank and his ''child'' King Oil. In Hank's world, he was absolute ruler. If you weren't with him, then you were against him.

Which is why Striker had been so sure Hank had written him off. That and the fact that the old man had vowed to disown him the last time he'd seen him, after the disastrous nineteenth birthday party Hank had thrown for Striker. In fact, Hank had shouted the words, tossing the threat at him as if throwing hand grenades. His face had been taut with rage, his oversized fists clenched.

Not the picture of the loving grandfather. But there
had been other moments, when Hank had taught Striker
how to bait a hook and taken him fishing, that had given
Striker hope that there might have been a bond forged
between them.

He'd never know now....

Striker turned off the memories and refocused his attention on Kate.

The bottom line was that this lady lawyer, with her
fancy ways and arrogant assumptions that he'd obediently fall in with his grandfather's plans, represented that
wealthy lifestyle—the one that Striker had so painfully
collided with that summer.

Oh, yeah, he had plenty of reasons to be upset.

But he didn't know why she had eyed him so disap-
provingly, calling him a stubborn Marine. Her voice had
a new edge to it, an edge that got him wondering what
her story was.

"How many Marines have you dealt with?" he asked.

"Not many," she admitted. "But I know your type."

"Really? And what type might that be, ma'am?" he
drawled, noticing for the first time how lush her mouth
was.

"The type that takes pleasure in living on the edge.
The type that never feels more alive than when you're
risking your life."

"Is that a crime?"

Kate wanted to answer that it should be. But that
would mean revealing too much about her inner feelings,
so she bit her tongue and stayed silent instead.

"How long were you Hank's attorney?" he demanded.

"Why do you care?" she countered.

"Just answer the question."

"Two years. Before that my father had been his attorney for a number of years. But my father had a heart attack and was required to cut back his workload, so I took over several of his clients, including Mr. King.''

Striker wondered what she was thinking, wondered what was going on behind those cool blue eyes of hers. He preferred doing that to dealing with his own torn emotions—the unexpected grief at knowing he was never going to make peace with his grandfather, the conflicting resentment toward the old man for manipulating him even from the grave.

He had to view this entire mess as if it were just another special op. Get in, accomplish the mission, get out.

But none of his missions had ever tugged at his emotions this way.

Sure, he'd been affected by some of the things he'd seen over the years. But you packaged it up, put it on the shelf and got on with the job.

Good advice. He needed to do that here.

Striker had a feeling that would not be easy in this case.

Not that Marines were into easy. No, difficult was their specialty. A good Marine loves a challenge. And Kate was certainly a challenge.

Under other circumstances he might even have enjoyed flirting with her. If she hadn't acted so icy and above him.

"I made our return travel arrangements before I left Texas," she said. "We're booked on a flight to San Antonio tonight."

Okay, this was another thing that aggravated him about her. "Sure of yourself, aren't you."

Kate wished that was the case, but it wasn't. Not at all. Striker could disrupt her normal calmness with remarkable ease. Which was why she'd wrapped her Ice

Queen mantle around herself for protection. Who wouldn't be rattled by coming face-to-face with the man who'd been the source of so many of her secret sexual fantasies, forbidden fantasies.

But there was more to it than that. So much more…

The bottom line was that Kate hadn't anticipated this…thing…this *physical* thing that seemed to exist between them.

Just passing by him when he'd held the door open for her had made her heart beat twice as fast. Sitting at the large conference table with him now made her breath catch. And she had yet to even touch him. Not that she planned on doing that. But it was bound to happen at some point.

Maybe it would be best if she got it over with right now. Waiting for it only made things worse.

She dropped her pen, which obediently rolled across the table toward him. Striker picked it up, but instead of handing it over to her, he tossed it onto the yellow legal pad she'd taken out of her briefcase.

Was he deliberately avoiding touching her? Why?

She tried to imagine herself in his shoes—discovering that a member of her family had died, someone with whom she'd never made her peace. She'd be a wreck. She'd been a wreck when her father had had his heart attack two years ago.

But Striker was different. For one thing, he was a guy and guys dealt with these things differently. He was also a Marine, which no doubt meant he was even more disciplined about not showing any emotion.

Maybe she should be a little more understanding. "I'm sorry things have worked out this way, Striker."

It was the first time she'd said his name and the sound of it on her lips made his heart unexpectedly clench. His strong reaction to her caught him by surprise. This particular female had a way of getting under his skin. Not a good sign. So he did what any good Marine would do. He fought back. "I don't need your pity."

She flinched as if he'd struck her. Great, now he had more guilt to add to the mess.

Concentrate on the mission, he grimly ordered himself. But it didn't work. Not with her sitting so close that he could hear her breathe, could smell her rich perfume, could see the way her tongue darted out to nervously lick her lower lip.

He reached for the pitcher of cold water that stood in the center of the table. So did she. His hand covered hers. Her skin was so soft. He could feel her fingers tremble like soft butterflies against his callused palm.

Kate reminded herself about that old adage of being careful what you wished for. She'd wondered what touching him would be like. Now she knew. It was incredibly powerful.

Sexual awareness shot like a lightning bolt up her arm, infusing her entire body with hot restlessness and forbidden thoughts.

No, she wasn't doing this. She wasn't getting involved. Not with Striker. No way, no how. He triggered memories much too painful to relive.

She slid her hand from his so suddenly the water pitcher almost tipped over.

Anger rushed over her, surprising her with its intensity. He was just a Marine, she bitterly reminded herself, another risk-taking adrenaline junkie who lived to cheat death. In the end, Striker and her former fiancé weren't that different after all. Except that Striker was still alive…and Ted wasn't.

There was no changing the past, but she wasn't going to make the same mistake twice. She was going to keep her relationship with Striker *strictly* professional—no matter what it took.

Chapter Two

Striker stood in the bedroom of his furnished rental apartment near the base, jamming a few of his belongings into his seabag with one hand while pressing the memory dial button on his cell phone with the other. Kate was waiting outside for him in a cab.

After years as a Force Recon Marine, Striker was well accustomed to deploying on a moment's notice. But he wasn't accustomed to doing so in regard to his family.

Fighting for freedom or justice was something he could manage. He didn't know how to manage telling his mom about his grandfather's death.

Striker considered telling his dad the news and having his dad tell his mom. But the bottom line was that Stan Kozlowski was no better at this kind of thing than Striker was. In fact, he may even have been worse.

"Hello?"

He smiled at the sound of his mother's soft-spoken voice. Many were deceived by her sweet demeanor, which camouflaged a will of steel. Angela King Kozlowski needed to be strong to be a Marine's wife, to marry him against her father's wishes and to raise five sons of her own. He and his brothers would walk on hot coals for her.

"Hello?" Angela repeated. "Is there anyone there?"

"Hey, Mom, it's Striker." He could hear the sound of the ocean in the background. "Where are you?"

"Eating lunch along the Oregon coast. It's really lovely out here, Striker. You should visit this area sometime."

"Yeah, maybe I will." He figured he'd stalled long enough. "Listen, Mom, I've got some bad news."

"Is it your brothers? Are they okay?"

Striker cursed under his breath at the fear in his mother's voice. He should have started differently. "No, it's not my brothers. We're all fine. It's your father. I'm sorry, Mom, I just found out that he's passed away. Heart attack. In his sleep, so he didn't suffer."

She was silent.

Striker swore silently. He shouldn't have just spit it out like that. He should have worked up to it gently. Sure, his mother was a steel magnolia, but even she was bound to be upset by news like this. She might be strong, but she also had a softer side. "Mom, are you okay?"

"Yes," she said quietly. "It's just a surprise. Somehow I thought he'd always be down there in Texas, running King Oil."

"Yeah, well, about King Oil…it seems that he didn't disown us the way we thought." He told her about the terms of the will as briefly as he could.

"I had no idea my father was planning something like this," his mom said. "How do you feel about it all, Striker?"

"I'm ready to obey my orders."

"Of course you are. But that wasn't what I asked."

Striker tossed in his shaving kit before closing his seabag. His mom wasn't just tough yet caring, she was also incredibly astute. She could probably sense that he was upset about this turn of events, despite his best efforts to hide that from her.

He loved his mom, but there was no way he was talking about his emotions with her. He hadn't done that since he was ten and he sure wasn't about to start now. "Listen, I've got to go, Mom. I'm sorry to be giving you such bad news about your father."

"What about the funeral? When will it be?"

"Funeral?" Striker repeated, not even having thought of that.

"He didn't want the fuss of a funeral," Kate said from behind him, startling him. "He had a private burial earlier this week."

Striker couldn't believe Kate had slipped past his customary awareness of his surroundings. As a Force Recon Marine, his very survival depended on him being able to keep his head at all times, in all circumstances.

He'd dealt with combat situations. He'd completed surgical strikes in the dead of night. He'd successfully executed search-and-destroy operations. So why was one rich blonde throwing him?

"Let me get back to you on that, Mom. We'll talk again soon." Jabbing the end call button, he tossed his phone aside to glare at Kate. "What are you doing in here?"

"I was wondering how much longer you'd be? Our flight leaves in two hours, we really should be at the airport right now."

"You've never heard of knocking before you enter a place?"

"I did knock, you didn't answer. The door was ajar, so I came in."

Leaving doors open? Striker *never* did that. Another sign that he didn't have his head screwed on straight at the moment.

He narrowed his gaze on her, trying to figure out exactly what it was about her that was getting to him. She was pretty, but he'd dealt with pretty women before. Quite successfully.

She was classy and wealthy.

Okay, those were things he tended to avoid in his women.

Not that he went for trashy girls. But the ones born with a silver spoon in their mouths tended to hit him the wrong way. It didn't take a psychiatrist to figure out why.

He'd turned nineteen during that summer he'd spent with his grandfather in Texas. His grandfather had thrown a big party, big in the way only Texans know how to accomplish. Wanting to show off, his grandfather had chosen a superexclusive country club as the location.

The entire thing had been a disaster as far as Striker was concerned. Not at first. At first, he'd been flattered by the attention of all the girls. What hormone-driven male of that age wouldn't have been?

He'd been pursuing one girl in particular, Carolyn Sinclair, for weeks. Like Kate, she'd been a sexy blonde with long legs and a lot of class. He'd been dancing with her, real close, when his grandfather had stopped the music to make the announcement that Striker would be joining him at King Oil.

Striker had been stunned. He'd been upfront with his grandfather from the get-go. Striker was following in his father's proud footsteps and becoming a Marine. No way was he becoming an oilman.

To this day, Striker could still vividly remember the horrified look on everyone's face when he'd joined Hank at the podium only to contradict his grandfather's words. Striker had agreed to spend the summer to please his mother, he'd told the crowd, but his plans remained unchanged. Striker was joining the U.S. Marines.

The attitude of the crowd changed faster than a prairie fire with a tailwind.

The girls, with their big hair and even bigger bank accounts, had turned their backs on him. As for sweet Carolyn...well, she'd told him what a loser he was in no uncertain terms, throwing a hissy fit in front of everyone, shouting that the only reason she'd bothered to spend any time at all on a redneck like him was because of his grandfather's money. So much for her ''classy'' ways.

Yeah, it was safe to say that the entire thing had left a very bad taste in his mouth and the desire to distance himself entirely from rich chicks born with silver spoons in their mouths.

His gaze settled on Kate. Unfortunately there was no distancing himself from this rich chick. He was stuck with her.

Kate wondered what she'd done to aggravate Striker this time. He was staring at her with those intense green eyes of his. There was no reading this guy's thoughts. He was a pro at disguising them. But the aggravation, *that* came through loud and clear.

She shifted her attention away from the brooding Marine and instead glanced around the studio apartment.

She suspected it was a furnished rental. Aside from a glimpse of a few brightly colored Hawaiian shirts hanging in the almost-empty closet, there was nothing much to give her any additional insight into Striker's character. The only personal items were two framed photos on the dresser. One looked to be of his family—his parents and brothers—and the other appeared to be a beach house of some kind.

The room was all done in monochromatic beiges, except for the bold Native American colors of the comforter on the neatly made bed. Her eyes remained on the bed while her mind wandered into forbidden territory.

Did Striker sleep on his back or on his side? Did he sleep in the nude? She imagined the sheet falling around his waist...

She reined in her wayward thoughts. Oh, no, she wasn't starting this again. Having fantasies about Striker. Absolutely not. This was where she'd gotten into trouble in the first place.

Closing her eyes, the memories came fast and hard. After mooning about Striker for most of the summer, four months later, on her eighteenth birthday in late December she'd delighted her parents by saying yes to golden-boy Ted Wentworth's marriage proposal. She and Ted had practically grown up together. Their parents were best friends and had made no secret of their desire for their only children to join together in holy matrimony.

The only son of one of Texas's wealthiest families, Ted was two years older than Kate and an inveterate risk taker, participating in extreme sports like heli-snowboarding in the winter and race-car driving in the summer. But despite the fact that Ted was an adrenaline junkie, being with him had never made her heart beat wildly the way watching Striker had.

During her six-month engagement to Ted, Kate had tried to forget about Striker, who'd left Texas to join the Marines. But the fantasies she'd had that steamy summer had stubbornly remained fixed in her mind throughout the ensuing months, coming out at night to possess her dreams.

One recurring theme had her leaving Ted at the altar and running off with the sexy, rebellious Striker. Striker, who'd followed his dream of joining the Marines. Striker, who'd pleased himself instead of others.

Logically she'd told herself that Striker merely represented freedom.

Freedom was something she couldn't afford right now. Because whenever she tried to follow her dreams, disaster struck. People died.

So Kate had wrapped up all her dreams and put them away, focusing instead on stability. That was the thing she valued most these days.

She couldn't allow being with Striker to distract her from that fact.

"We'd better get going," she said with chilly briskness, falling back into her Ice Queen persona. "We've got a plane to catch."

Striker had flown to war-torn countries faster than his trip to San Antonio. Everything that could have gone wrong did. Their flight was delayed umpteen times before being cancelled altogether. Bad weather was snarling up the entire system.

They were finally put on another flight and the plane actually left the gate, only to sit for another ninety minutes on the runway. By the time they'd arrived in San Antonio it was almost midnight. Luckily their luggage hadn't gotten messed up, but then he only had his carry-on seabag and Kate only had her briefcase and purse.

A company car was waiting for them. After scrunching his six-two body into a cramped airplane seat, Striker was infinitely glad for the limo with ample room.

He glanced over to where Kate had fallen asleep, her head resting on his shoulder. She'd taken some kind of travel sickness pills that had completely zonked her out. He'd barely gotten her into the limo before she was out again.

In fact, he'd been so concerned with keeping Kate upright and not sliding into a boneless heap on the sidewalk at the terminal, that he wasn't even sure where they were headed now.

But when the limo eventually turned off the main road onto a long one-lane drive, Striker knew. They were heading for Westwind, his grandfather's ranch.

Not his first choice, but at this point he was too tired to care. Besides, he had a bigger problem at the moment. Kate.

"How many of those pills did you take?" Striker muttered as Kate slid half-across his lap. His hand landed on her nylon-clad thigh.

His body reacted accordingly to the feel of a sexy woman strewn across it. He was still wearing his uniform, but that didn't stop his arousal from hardening beneath the placket of his khaki pants.

As the car rolled to a smooth stop, Striker had a decision to make. Leave an out-of-it Kate in the limo with directions for the driver to take her home—not that he knew where that was—or take her inside with him.

He carried her inside.

The white pillars standing guard on either side of the door made the place look more like the White House than a Western ranch. But then his grandfather always had been into power and the White House image evoked a lot of power.

The front door opened, and there stood ranch foreman Tony Martinez, his now-white, thick hair standing on end instead of smoothly slicked back as it had been the last time he'd seen him twelve years ago. His face reflected the outdoor life he led.

"Did we wake you, Tony? The fuzzy bunny slippers are a nice touch," Striker added, looking down.

Tony grinned sheepishly. "I forgot I was wearing them. It is good to see you again." Then he noticed the woman in Striker's arms and his expression became concerned. "What happened?"

"Nothing a good night's rest won't cure," Striker replied, moving past Tony to head for the grand staircase. "Kate took one of those motion sickness pills and it's zonked her. Are the bedrooms still upstairs?"

Tony nodded and led the way. The expensive Oriental carpet runners softened the sound of Striker's footsteps as he mounted the steps and efficiently made his way to the closest guest bedroom. There were five in the house.

After placing Kate on the bed, still without a word from her other than a ladylike sigh, Striker turned to Tony. "Is Maria still the housekeeper here?"

"No, her daughter Consuela is housekeeper now. But she's not here today. She had to visit her mother in the hospital in Corpus Christi. That's why I'm here in the house instead of over at the foreman's place."

"Are you the only one here?"

Tony nodded.

"We have to get her ready for bed," Striker said with a nod down at Kate.

"Ready for bed? No, this is not something I do." Tony hurriedly backed out of the room. "I will see you downstairs." He paused on the threshold before turning back to narrow his dark eyes at Striker. "I can trust you to behave as a gentleman, *si?* Not to take advantage of Señorita Kate?"

"You can trust me, Tony."

The foreman nodded briskly. *"Bueno."*

A second later, Striker was alone in the softly lit bedroom with Kate.

Plan, prepare, execute. These were the steps a Marine took to accomplish his mission.

Tonight Striker's mission was to prepare Kate for bed. Which meant removing her shoes.

Check.

What about nylons?

He needed more information. If they were pantyhose…

They weren't.

Okay, then. Speedy decision making was one of the signs of a good Marine, and Striker was a very good Marine.

Removing nylons.

Check.

It was getting hotter than a tropical jungle in here. That's why his fingers trembled slightly after he peeled the sheer nylons off her long legs.

Kate mumbled and nearly poked his eye out with her knee as she rolled onto her side.

Now the curve of her hip drew his attention. So did her bare thighs, exposed by the hiked-up hem of her skirt. He knew firsthand how incredibly soft her skin was.

He shifted his attention to a less provocative area.

He probably should remove her suit jacket. Striker undid the first two buttons, not knowing what he'd find beneath. What he found was a lacy black bra that made his heart stop.

The temperature in the room rose another twenty degrees. The last button on the jacket was proving to be especially stubborn. The backs of his fingers brushed against her breast as he struggled—struggled to breathe.

She cuddled closer.

His breathing stopped. His body throbbed.

He got the last button undone and temporarily retreated.

Okay, he had to be fast about this, because drawing things out was only prolonging the sexual torture.

Jacket and then skirt removed efficiently.

Check.

She was wearing a slip. Black like her bra.

Fine, she could keep wearing it.

Because he'd had enough for one evening.

Striker grabbed a comforter from the chest at the foot of the bed and covered her with it, from chin to toe. Then he hightailed it out of the room.

He was greeted by Tony at the foot of the stairs.

"Señorita Kate is okay?"

Striker nodded. "Yeah, she'll be fine. She took some new kind of travel sickness pill that knocked her out. She'll be fine," he repeated. Striker wasn't so sure about himself, however. His body still ached. What kind of pervert was he to get so aroused over an unconscious woman's half-naked body?

Yeah, well, Striker had never claimed to be a saint.

He deliberately focused his attention on the ranch foreman. "Like I said before, Tony, those are mighty nice slippers."

"They are a gift from my granddaughter. They keep my poor feet warm."

"Your feet warm? It's early September. The average temperature down here this time of year is in the mid-eighties." Or so he'd discovered when surfing the Internet for information on King Oil and San Antonio while waiting for their flight to board. Kate wasn't the only one who knew how to use a laptop. He'd tossed his into his seabag at the last minute.

"It's cooler at night." Tony's expression turned stubborn.

"Yeah, when it gets down to seventy. Big deal."

Tony waved his words away. "You don't have grand-children, so you don't understand."

"How many do you have now?" Striker asked.

"Six."

Normally Striker wasn't the kind to make small talk, but it prevented him from dealing with other stuff—like the fact that Kate turned him on.

His gaze settled on the foyer, where a large portrait of his grandfather hung. Hank King gazed out at the world as if daring anyone to mess with him.

Regrets washed over Striker—regret that time had run out, that he and his grandfather had never made peace, that his grandfather was no longer with them. True, he hadn't agreed with the old man, but he had never wanted him dead.

Unable to breathe, Striker quickly moved out the French doors to the patio that ran along the back of the house. The lights illuminating the large swimming pool couldn't compete with the sparkle of stars above. He'd traveled around the world but had always remembered the night sky here at the ranch as being something special.

"I didn't think you'd come back," Tony admitted.

"Believe me, it wasn't *my* idea."

"I know. It was your grandfather's idea. That's why I didn't think you'd come."

"I'm just following orders. The Marine Corps's orders, not my grandfather's orders."

"In this case, they are one and the same, *si?*"

Striker nodded. He'd had always known that this wasn't the life for him, that he'd have no freedom with his dictatorial grandfather calling all the shots. Yet here he was, doing what his grandfather wanted and returning to Texas.

At times like this Striker was convinced Fate was a female, and that she was laughing her head off at this Force Recon Marine.

Chapter Three

"This is a surprise," Kate's father noted as he looked at her over the top of the morning paper. This morning, as he did every morning, Jack Bradley was eating breakfast in the formal dining room with its sumptuous red walls and gilded mirror. Her mother had one of San Antonio's best interior decorators design the area to her specifications—which were *rich* and *richer*. "I thought you were still in Washington."

"I got back late last night. Is that coffee?" Kate slid into a chair and reached for the thermal carafe. She'd walked the mile between Westwind and her parents' place. Her Italian shoes would never be the same again.

"Of course it's coffee," he replied. "What else would I be drinking in the morning?"

"Decaf?"

"Yes, unfortunately. Doctor's orders."

"When is your next appointment with your heart doctor?"

"You sound like your mother." He eyed her critically. "I must say you're looking rather rumpled this morning."

Kate wasn't about to tell him that that was because she'd spent the night next door. "I ended up on a red-eye flight last night. I didn't plan it that way, but we kept running into flight delays…"

"By your use of the term *we* I'm assuming that you brought Hank's grandson back with you?"

"His name is Striker, and I didn't *bring* him with me, he came with me. He's a Marine and they don't take kindly to being *brought* anywhere."

"Because he's a Marine, I would assume he'd be accustomed to taking orders," her father said, crisply folding the newspaper in half and setting it on the table. "Did he give you any problems?"

Plenty of them, she thought, but they were not the type that she could talk about with her father.

Kate still wasn't sure how she ended up in the guest bedroom with half her clothes undone. She prayed that the housekeeper had put her to bed, but she had a vague recollection of turning over and seeing Striker looming above her.

Maybe that had been a dream. Surely, he wouldn't take off her clothes?

What was she thinking? Of course he'd take off her clothes. He was a guy, wasn't he?

But he was a Marine. Weren't they supposed to have a higher code of honor or something?

Which meant that if he did undo some of her clothing, he would have done so with his eyes closed.

Yeah, right.

"Well?" her father prompted her. "Were there problems?"

"Nothing I can't manage."

"I certainly hope that's the case." Her father didn't sound very confident of her competency. But then that was vintage Jack Bradley. No one could meet the high standards he set, not only for others but for himself as well. "I don't understand why Hank insisted that you handle this matter yourself."

"Because he had faith in my abilities."

Jack picked up a dry piece of toast, glared at it and then tossed it back on the plate. "I should be the one handling his estate."

"You already have more than enough work to deal with," Kate reminded him. "The doctor told you that you had to cut back on the number of hours you spend at the office."

"And I've done that."

"I know you have. Honestly, I can handle things with the King estate. You don't have to worry about a thing."

"Hmm." He made his customary noncommittal murmur which really meant *I don't buy that for one minute.*

"Kate!" Her mother's voice sounded horrified as she entered the room with her customary elegance. Even this early in the morning Elizabeth Hunter Bradley was the epitome of good grooming, wearing silk pants the color of café au lait along with a designer paisley blouse in swirls of browns. As a former Miss Texas she took great pride in her looks, and took great care to maintain them. "You look like something the cat dragged in."

"We don't have a cat," Kate replied, rather pleased at how calm she sounded given the fact that her stomach was in knots. Kate may have inherited her mother's blond hair and blue eyes, but she lacked her mother's innate ability to achieve perfection.

"You know very well what I mean." Now her mother

sounded irritated. "What on earth happened to you? You look as if you've slept in that suit."

"She had a bad flight in from Washington," her father replied on her behalf.

"What is she doing here at this time in the morning?" Her mother poured herself a cup of coffee. "Shouldn't she be getting ready for work?"

"I'm right here," Kate reminded her parents. "I can hear you talking about me."

"Then answer the question," her mother said.

"I'm hoping Dad can give me a ride into the city this morning," Kate said.

"Why do you need a ride?" her mother asked.

"Because my car is still at my condo. So are my clothes."

"And why aren't you there?" Her mother continued the inquisition.

"Because the limo from the airport dropped me off out here." Kate was not about to admit that she'd spent the night at Hank's ranch with Striker, that he'd possibly put her to bed, removing half her clothes. Let her parents think she'd just gotten in from the airport.

"Dropped you off out here? Why would the driver do that?" her mother said.

"There was a mix-up. Oh, my, look at the time." Kate made a big deal of tapping her fourteen-karat gold watch, a present from her father. "We'd better be going, Dad."

"Right."

Thankfully her father only talked about business during the drive into the city where he'd agreed to drop her off at her condo. He made no further reference to Striker.

That didn't mean Kate wasn't thinking about Striker, however. And wondering if she'd only dreamt the magic of his touch on her breasts last night....

* * *

"May I help you, sir?" The woman behind the reception desk on the top floor of King Oil's headquarters eyed him warily.

Striker couldn't blame her. He knew he looked out of place. He didn't own a suit, not that he'd wear one if he could at all avoid it.

And he wasn't sure of Marine procedure for wearing his uniform in this case. Sure he was here as a result of his commanding officer's request that he do so. But did this really qualify as Marine business?

He'd settled for jeans and a denim shirt. Standard attire in Texas. But not, apparently, on the executive floor of King Oil's headquarters, if the receptionist's frown was any gauge.

"Good morning, ma'am." He flashed his best smile at the suspicious receptionist. "I'm Striker Kozlowski."

"Oh, Mr. King's grandson. I'm so sorry, sir! I didn't know it was you." The woman was practically trembling in her shoes.

"No problem," he assured her as she ushered him in past the frosted glass doors that led to the executive offices.

Striker remembered visiting King Oil's San Antonio headquarters the one summer he'd spent with his grandfather before joining the Marines. He never thought he'd set foot in this place again.

Midland or Houston were the more customary locations for an oilman's headquarters, but then his grandfather had never been one to follow the crowd. He'd taken a shine to San Antonio and had decided to set up business there. End of story. Or the beginning of it.

His grandfather's office suite was at the end of the wide hall. A massive desk stood guard outside the inner sanctum. He paused several feet away to assess the situation...and to appreciate the young woman standing beside the desk. She could have been a lingerie model. She was petite and busty with long red hair that reached halfway down her back. Her short skirt showed plenty of leg.

For the first time since this thing had started, Striker felt optimistic. Maybe this mission wouldn't be so difficult after all.

The metal nameplate on her desk said she was Tex Murphy.

She didn't look like a Tex to him, but he didn't really care what her name was. He was just standing there enjoying the view when he heard Kate's voice by his side. "Good morning, Striker."

"Yes, it is," he agreed, keeping his eyes on sexy Tex. "Was Tex Murphy my grandfather's assistant?"

"Yes. She'll be your assistant, as well."

"Great."

"But that's not Tex," Kate informed him.

"What do you mean?"

"I mean the young woman you're drooling over is not Tex Murphy."

"Marines do not drool," Striker stated, swiveling his gaze to Kate.

"Right."

"You, standing over there by Kate, state your business," a grouchy, gravelly voice demanded.

Striker's dreams of being pampered by the sexy redhead dissolved. "Let me guess. That's Tex."

"Yes, it is," Kate said cheerfully.

There's no way anyone would mistake Tex for a lingerie model. She did have a lot in common with a drill sergeant, however, including the voice. She was a petite little thing, but she had the bearing of a general. Her short hair was gun-metal gray and her light blue eyes reflected her dissatisfaction.

"Is she always this grouchy or is she just not a morning person?" Striker asked.

"Tex is always this way," Kate replied with a smile that told him she was taking great satisfaction in this.

"Great."

"Don't tell me a big bad Marine like you is afraid of a spitfire like Tex?"

"Marines are never afraid," he stated.

"I'm glad to hear that."

Striker decided she was having entirely too much fun at his expense. Time to turn the tables on her. "So where did you disappear to this morning?"

"This is not the time to discuss that," she noted with a meaningful look in Tex's direction.

"Don't tell me a big bad attorney like you is afraid of a spitfire like Tex?" he mocked her.

"Tex has ears and eyes in the back of her head," Kate muttered.

"I heard that," Tex growled. "So you two might as well get yourselves on over here and talk to me directly instead of behind my back."

"Yes, ma'am." Striker said before flashing her a grin. "Striker Kozlowski at your service, ma'am."

"I sincerely doubt that," Tex retorted.

"Doubt what? That I'm Striker?"

"That you're at my service. That you're up to no good, now that I'd believe."

"Ma'am I'm just here to…" To what? He regrouped. "To assess the situation."

"I can tell you the situation. Your grandfather, God bless his soul, has cashed in his chips and departed this earth. For some reason he saw fit to complicate all our lives by demanding that you, a Marine, spend time pretending to be an oilman in charge of a huge company. Luckily you've got me to help you."

"I'm sure you'll be an invaluable asset, ma'am," Striker noted solemnly.

Her narrow gaze was filled with suspicion. "I hope you're not fixin' to be messin' with my routine around here."

"I wouldn't dream of it," Striker assured her.

"I hope you *are* fixin' to be messin' with some other folks' routines. They won't take kindly to that, an outsider like you comin' in here and messin' with things." She gave him an assessing head-to-toe look. "But then you don't appear to be the sort of man to walk away from a fight."

"I'm a Marine, ma'am. We don't walk away from fights."

"And they're never afraid," Kate added with a grin. "He already told me that much."

"Anything else I should know about Marines?" Tex demanded.

"Plenty, but we don't have to go into all the details this morning."

"Just remember you're in Texas now."

"Hard to forget that, ma'am," Striker noted with a nod toward the huge map of the state on one wall.

"And Texans are different."

"By different, she means better," Kate said.

"Shoot, I would have thought that much was obvious." Tex said.

"I can't work here," Striker growled in frustration an hour later. He stood in his grandfather's office. Before him were the floor-to-ceiling windows offering a great view of the skyline. The San Antonio River with its well-known River Walk meandered through the city while the Alamo rested in solitude to one side.

Striker felt like those men stuck in the Alamo, fighting

against incredible odds. Not only was Kate inundating him with information about the company, but he was surrounded by the presence of his grandfather.

The walls were filled with photos of Hank standing beside former and present leaders of the free world. A pair of bronzes by some famous Western artist, Kate had told him the name but he'd forgotten, were on either side of a dark green leather couch that would have seated five comfortably.

There were no photos of family on Hank's desk or anywhere in the office. No personal items. Only indicators of power. And a mural of oil rigs painted on the far wall that had at its core a saying by fellow oilman John Paul Getty—"Success: Rise early, work hard, strike oil."

Striker supposed Hank had done all that. But what did he really know of his grandfather? There were few clues here.

Pausing at the desk, Striker reached out to touch the fountain pen sitting there. This he did remember. Hank had never liked ball-point pens. He'd been old-fashioned in his preference for fountain pens. And for baiting his hooks with handmade lures he'd devised himself.

It was as if everything had been left just as it was, waiting for Hank to return. Only he wasn't returning.

Striker wasn't listening to a word Kate was saying, and he needed to. This was important. He needed to be successful in this mission. But to do so, he had to make some changes.

Striker strode to the door and called out to Tex. "I need a conference room to set up my ops H.Q."

"You want to speak English?" Tex said.

"A conference room. To set up my operational headquarters."

"What are you fixin' to operate on?"

"This company."

"There's a meeting room down the hall to the right."

"Affirmative." He resorted to his military language. It made him feel more in control.

Ten minutes later he and Kate were seated in a small conference room.

"Don't you think you're being a little ridiculous by refusing to use your grandfather's office?" Kate said.

"Ridiculous?"

The tone of his voice should have warned her that she was entering dangerous waters, but it was too late now. "I just meant that it would be simpler to review the company's status in his office where we would have easy access to files."

"Marines aren't into easy."

"I'm learning that."

"This laptop computer is supposed to be able to access any information I need, so what's the problem?"

The problem was proximity. Unlike yesterday when she and Striker had sat across from one another at a conference table, today she had to sit beside him to show him how to use the spreadsheets displayed on the laptop computer.

The conference room he'd chosen was one of the smallest on this floor. Her shoulder kept bumping against his, her arm warmed by his body heat.

He was wearing jeans today, which reminded her of those times she'd seen him wearing jeans—and nothing else—that summer.

Or there was that first time, when he'd been skinny-dipping down by the pond. Wearing nothing at all.

She really had to get a grip here. She couldn't keep allowing her thoughts to stray. They were discussing important topics, subjects that affected the livelihood and well-being of hundreds of people.

What had they been talking about before she'd gone off the deep end? Oh, yes. Striker had asked her if there was a problem using the laptop computer.

"No problem," she belatedly replied. Which was a total lie of course. There were problems galore. Like her inability to keep her mind on business. Or the fact that Striker was getting more irritable by the minute.

"Who was that sexy redhead?" he asked out of the blue.

"Pardon me?" Kate blinked at him. Here she was having fantasies about Striker and he was interested in a redhead?

"That sexy redhead who was seated at Tex's desk earlier. Who is she?"

"Tex's granddaughter. I wouldn't recommend messing with her. Tex is very protective of her family."

"What makes you think I'd do anything Tex wouldn't approve of?"

"Experience."

"You don't have much experience with me."

True, but what experience she had had was definitely memorable. Except for her losing her clothing last night. That part was still hazy.

"Did you undress me last night?" she demanded abruptly.

"Define *undress.*"

"Don't dance around the question."

"Marines don't dance around questions."

"Fine, then answer it. Was Consuela the one who put me to bed last night?"

"I carried you upstairs to the bedroom, not Consuela."

"But then Consuela came and took things from there, right?" Kate said hopefully.

"No, ma'am. Consuela was in Corpus Christi last night visiting her mom. That left Tony and me."

"So you were the one who undressed me?"

"What makes you think it wasn't Tony?" Striker countered.

"He's too much of a gentleman."

"I thought I was being a gentleman by making you more comfortable."

"You thought wrong."

"Not a surprise. You always seem to think I'm doing the wrong thing. You've acted that way from the second you walked into my C.O.'s office in Quantico."

"Me? You're the one who isn't the happy camper, the one who made it clear that you didn't want to leave the Marines to come down here, that you think this entire idea is worthless. And now you throw a hissy fit and won't even work in your grandfather's office."

"Marines do *not* have hissy fits!" Striker growled.

"I wouldn't have minded if being surrounded by your grandfather's things was making you remember him too vividly and causing your grief to overwhelm you. But I doubt that was the case. You haven't shown the least bit of emotion about Hank's death. He was a good man."

"He was a dictatorial control freak calling all the shots."

"How dare you insult him now that he isn't here to defend himself!"

"Listen, you know nothing about me or how I feel so don't go thinking you're suddenly an expert on what I'm thinking. And don't go singing his praises to me. He turned his back on my mother when she needed him most. She was struggling with kids to raise. Money was tight, Marines don't make much, but Hank wouldn't lift a finger to help her out. He made things rough for her when he could have made them easier.'' There, the words were finally out.

Instead of agreeing with him, Kate asked, ''Did she ever ask him for help?''

''Of course not.''

''Well, then how could he know she'd need it?''

Her answer infuriated him. She sat there so cool and calm, so distant on her pedestal where she remained untouched by worries about making a paycheck stretch. ''There's no talking to you!'' He turned the swiveling conference chair to glare at her.

She did the same, moving her chair to glare at him, not backing down one inch. *''Me?* I'm not the one with issues. You are.''

''You don't know what you're talking about.'' Striker didn't realize how close they were until he felt her sweet breath bouncing off his lips. He saw the emotion flaring in her eyes—anger followed by sudden awareness.

It was too late to retreat, too late to think. Striker could only act, leaning forward just enough to capture her wayward mouth with his own.

Chapter Four

Kate hadn't expected Striker to kiss her. She didn't have time to prepare her defenses before he was already storming them.

His approach was forceful but not in a frightening way. What *was* scary was the way he made her *feel*— all hot and shivery deep inside.

The warm pressure of his mouth tantalized her, tempted her, overwhelmed her. The gentle brush of his fingertips against her jawline was at odds with the masterful way he consumed her, arousing a passion within her that had lain buried since Ted's death.

But even Ted had never created this kind of response in her.

Striker claimed her mouth as if exploring for riches. Her lips parted willingly, allowing his tongue to slip inside and flick inquiringly with a sensuality that drove her wild.

French kissing. She'd never understood the appeal before. Now she could. Oh yes, *yes!*

Her lips opened even farther under his expert tutelage, following his lead, matching his demands.

She felt the thud of his heart beneath her hand, could feel the softness of his denim shirt beneath her fingertips and the warmth of his skin beneath. She was on fire, passion throbbing through her entire body.

Her knees went weak, making her melt against him. Sexual need pooled in all the feminine places in her body—her breasts, her pelvis—both of which were pressed tightly against his fully aroused hard body.

Out of control. She was completely out of control. And out of her league. Ted may have been a risk taker but he'd never made her feel as if she'd stepped off a plane without a parachute. He'd never made her feel reckless.

This had to stop. She had to stop. But it felt so good. Dangerously good.

Remember what happens whenever you go after what you want.

The thought shot through her mind, shattering the haze of pleasure like a hammer shattering glass.

A second later the kiss was over—she and Striker breaking it off at the same time.

Striker took several steps away from her. He hadn't expected Kate to respond the way she had—to melt in his arms, to part her lips and grant him entry. Her passion threw him. Then he remembered the last time a ritzy female had kissed him as if she'd meant it…only to later inform him that it was all an act. Carolyn Sinclair. His nineteenth birthday.

Sure, that had been a long time ago, but some things a guy didn't forget.

And yeah, he'd kissed plenty of women since then. But none of them born with a spoon in their mouth the way Kate had been. They tended not to have any interest in a Force Recon Marine. He'd seen the type in Washington, D.C. They had dollar signs in their eyes. The size of a guy's bank account was the most important thing to them.

So why would a wealthy lady lawyer like Kate go all hot on him?

Yeah, there were thrill-seeking Special Forces groupies who were turned on by guys because they were Force Recon Marines, but that clearly was not the case with Kate.

He could, however, see the big appeal for her being his newfound financial status. He needed a reason, he needed to get a handle on this out-of-control situation. "I get it. Hooking up with a lowly Marine with a chip on his shoulder wouldn't look very good on your resume, but the grandson of the founder of King Oil looks excellent, right?"

Kate stared at him with disbelief. "What are you accusing me of now?"

"That you only kissed me because of my connection to several million dollars."

She was furious. "I don't need the money. And I wasn't kissing you, *you* were kissing *me*."

"That dog's not gonna hunt," he retorted. "You were kissing me back and enjoying it. I know when a woman melts in my arms."

Her face turned red. "Know this. You're just an impossibly stubborn Marine who caught me by surprise. It won't happen again. Believe me, you don't have anything I'm interested in!"

Okay, so maybe that was a lie. Kate was interested in his body and his kisses. Or had been. Against her will. But that was before he'd accused her of being some kind of money-grabbing social climber. Now all she felt was anger.

"We have a working relationship, Mr. Kozlowski. Nothing else. You'd do well to remember that and act in a manner accordingly." Her words dripped ice.

"The same goes for you, ma'am."

His comment pierced the protective cloak she'd placed around her emotions. He was right. What had she been thinking, responding to his kiss that way? She should have tossed her laptop at him the second he'd touched her.

"I'm sorry," he said quietly, surprising her. "I shouldn't have said that. And you're right. I shouldn't have kissed you. Like you said, we have to work together."

Her anger diffused like a balloon that had suddenly had all the air let out of it.

"I'm sorry, too. I should have stopped you. But you caught me by surprise…and I…I was thinking of someone else." The words inadvertently tumbled out.

"Ouch." His voice was rueful. "That put me in my place. So who were you thinking of? An old beau?"

"My fiancé."

"I didn't know you were engaged. You're not wearing a ring."

"I'm not engaged now. He died a number of years ago."

"I'm sorry."

"So am I. Ted was a risk taker like you. Believe me, I've got no desire to get tangled up with another man who is an adrenaline junkie." Turning on her heel, Kate walked out of the room, leaving Striker erotically imagining what it would be like to be "tangled up" with a woman like her.

The steamy heat of the jungle was all around Striker. One false move and he'd be a dead man. He had to remain perfectly still, as he had for hours.

His face was blackened. So was his soul. He'd seen and done so much. Nothing that could be talked about, nothing that could be revealed. But nothing that could be forgotten, either.

Faces appeared out of nowhere, hands grabbing for him.

Striker fought back, sweat pouring off his face. His muscles bunched as he tossed one man after another off him. But there were too many of them.

The next thing Striker knew, he was being staked out in the hot sand, the sun beating down on him. He pulled against the restraints holding him down but couldn't get free.

Then *she* was there. Kate. Standing above him, looking all cool and calm.

"Believe me, I've got no desire to get tangled up with another man who is an adrenaline junkie," she told him.

Infuriated, Striker yanked free of the wrist manacles and tugged her down to him. She sprawled over his aroused body and kissed him as they rolled over and over in the hot sand....

Striker woke up as he landed on the floor with a thump.

Damn. He rubbed his right elbow. He'd been dreaming. About Kate. And had ended up rolling out of the bed.

He felt like an idiot. What kind of Force Recon Marine was he to hit the deck like a raw recruit?

Well, at the moment he was a fully aroused Force Recon Marine.

A cold shower took care of that. There was no point going back to bed, since it was almost daylight anyway.

Striker hated dreams. Most of the time he refused to acknowledge he even had them.

He'd never been the type to analyze stuff, unless it was data relating to a mission. But there was something about Kate that was different.

Women had never thrown him before. He'd found plenty of them attractive. But there had never been this curiosity to know more and this inability to remain focused.

Kate wasn't the first woman he'd known to throw his work as a Force Recon Marine in his face. Several women over the past decade thought they could seduce him away from the Corps, only to call him names when they couldn't succeed.

He'd always tried to be upfront with them. Had always tried to make the rules of engagement clear, even in his sexual relationships. He was a Marine first and foremost. He wasn't giving that up for any woman. He didn't have a regular nine-to-five job that allowed for long-term relationships.

Kate was right. She didn't need to get hooked up with him.

But that didn't stop him from wondering about the fiancé who had died. And it sure didn't stop him from remembering the taste of her parted lips, or the feel of Kate's lush body pressed against his.

"What do you know about Kate Bradley?" Striker asked Tony as the two men sat in the big kitchen, downing a plateful of Consuela's tasty *huevos rancheros* an hour later. Morning sunlight streamed through the windows onto the surface of the pine table that could seat a dozen easily. Everything at Westwind Ranch was larger than life, reflecting Hank King's philosophy that bigger was better.

But Striker wasn't consumed with thoughts of his grandfather this morning. He was consumed with Kate.

"What do you want to know?" Tony countered.

"She told me she was engaged once."

"*Si*, that is right."

Getting information from Tony was like pulling teeth out of a porcupine. But Striker wasn't about to give up. *Surrender* was not in this Marine's vocabulary. "What happened?"

"He died."

Striker gritted his teeth and reined in his impatience. He could tell by Tony's slight smile that the older man was enjoying yanking his chain. "How?"

"In a car crash. She was there."

"In the car?" Striker's chest tightened at the thought of her in a serious car accident.

"In the crowd."

"What crowd?"

"The crowd watching the race. Her fiancé liked racing cars. His family was very wealthy. He did not need the money. It was the thrill. He was always doing wild things. That last one, the car racing, killed him. Only days before their wedding. She was so young and pale at the funeral."

"When did this happen?"

"After that summer you were here. Maybe a year later. Maybe a little less."

Yet Kate still thought about her fiancé when she kissed Striker. She must have loved the guy a lot. And to have seen him die in front of her that way, that had to be rough.

Striker felt like a heel for being so hard on her. Maybe that's why she had that Ice Queen routine going on. To protect herself from guys like him. He could understand that.

Jeez, now he was analyzing her. Not like him at all.

"Why are you interested in Kate?" Tony asked him.

"Because we'll be working together for the two months I'm here. She's advising me on the extent of Hank's estate and business holdings."

"She sure left here in a hurry the other morning," Tony noted.

Striker shrugged and poured himself another mug of Consuela's delicious coffee.

"She must have walked all the way over to her parents' house. Must be over a mile," Tony said.

"That was her choice. She could have waited and gotten a ride from you or me."

"Bah!" Consuela exclaimed, entering the conversation for the first time. The housekeeper's dark hair was held back with a wide silver clip as she glared at them both with indignant brown eyes. "Men! They have no idea." She lifted her eyes heavenward before returning her gaze to them. "Señorita Kate would not wait after you put her to bed."

Striker gave Tony an accusing look.

Tony just shrugged. "I cannot lie to Consuela. She asked me why the guest room bed was used and I had to tell her."

"What did she threaten you with?" Striker retorted. "Coffee withdrawal?"

"Worse. She threatened not to make me any of her sopapilla. It is even better than her mother's."

Striker remembered the incredible fried pastry dessert served with honey that Maria used to make. "How is your mother?" Striker asked Consuela.

"*Bueno*. The eye surgery went well. She will soon be seeing better than ever before. Better than you two men who cannot see that a woman would be embarrassed by having to face the man who put her to bed the night before."

"Nothing happened to be embarrassed about. Other than Tony here wearing bunny slippers when we showed up."

Consuela was not distracted by Striker's comment. She stuck to her guns. "You cannot put yourself in her shoes?"

Striker shook his head.

"No way. She's a woman. I'm not."

Consuela grabbed their empty plates and marched off, muttering under her breath in rapid Spanish.

Put himself in Kate's size-six shoes? What did he know about how women thought? And he was certainly no expert in the love department. Give him something simple, like covert tactical maneuvers, any day.

Thinking about tactical maneuvers reminded him that he needed to deal with upper management at King Oil this morning. He'd be wise to keep his thoughts firmly centered on that and off of a certain lady lawyer who kissed like a sexy angel.

"What did you do to her?" Tex demanded as soon as Striker arrived at King Oil.

"To who?"

"To Kate. She lit out of here yesterday as if her hair was on fire."

There had definitely been some fire involved. When they kissed it had been instant combustion. Like a land mine, hitting you when you least expected it.

Striker should have known better. He'd felt the chemistry between them from the moment he'd first seen Kate back at Quantico. He'd chalked it up to resentment about her ritzy, bossy ways. But there had been more to it than that.

"You still haven't answered my question," Tex impatiently reminded him. "What did you do to Kate?"

He wasn't about to admit that he'd kissed her. Instead he said, "You don't have to worry about Kate."

"I do worry about her. I've known her and her family for a coon's age." Tex fixed him with a laser look. "You do anything to hurt her and you'll have to answer to me."

"I promise I'll be on my best behavior with her. Now can we get back to business? I want you to gather the executives together so I can talk to them."

"They're already together," Tex said. "In the large conference room."

"How did you know that's what I was planning for today?"

"I didn't. They had this meeting scheduled before you showed up. And they're having it without you."

"Who called the meeting?"

"Charles Longly, V.P. of Finance."

Striker remembered briefly meeting him yesterday, a tall man with a receding hairline and greedy eyes. Striker had overheard the guy talking to another executive, not realizing he was being overheard. "I think it's ridiculous that we have some grunt from the Marines coming in here and pretending to run things for two months," Charles had complained.

Oh, yeah, this grunt from the Marines remembered Charles Longly all right.

"Give me a quick wrap-up of your opinion of this guy," Striker told Tex.

"The sneaky sort of maneuverer. A weasel who prefers vice to advice," Tex noted tartly.

"Well now, if that isn't just too bad. Because I definitely feel like giving out some advice today. And I do believe I'll go do that right now in the large conference room."

"Here." She slapped a file folder in his hand. "This is their agenda for the meeting."

Charles was sitting at the head of the conference table, with his back to the door when Striker burst in unannounced. "You can't go in there…" a frazzled secretary guarding the outer doors said.

Striker ignored her. The huge conference room had the same view as his grandfather's office. It also had tons of food laid out. No paper cups of coffee for this crew. Only fine china and silver.

"Ah, there you are, Striker," Charles said as if he were in charge of things. "Since you're not familiar with business procedures, you might want to just sit down in the corner there and observe today's meeting until you've learned more about the company."

"That's not gonna happen," Striker said, strolling over to the catered goodies and popping a strawberry into his mouth. "It looks like you have all the luxuries here. And the executive head down the hall looks like something out of a palace," he noted, using the Marine terminology for bathroom. "Is that marble in there?"

"Finest Italian marble on the floors and walls as well as the counters," Charles noted proudly.

"Must have cost a pretty penny."

"Your grandfather believed in having only the best."

"At the expense of his people?" Striker countered.

"Excuse me?"

"I saw the annual reports. Now as you said, I'm not familiar with business procedures, but I saw that many of you received huge bonuses despite the fact that the company's net worth is lower now than it has been in years."

"The company is just going through a rough patch right now," Charles said defensively.

"And whose fault is that?" Striker said.

"There are a number of reasons for the economy…"

Striker interrupted him. "I'm not talking about the economy, I'm talking about this company. And about the policy of those at the top getting fat at the expense of the little guy at the bottom. You laid off workers as cost-cutting measures and you're threatening to lay off more."

"No offense intended, Striker…" Charles was using that condescending tone again, the one that made Striker want to punch his lights out. "But business management really isn't your field of expertise."

"Leadership is my field of expertise."

"Perhaps, but we aren't in the Marine Corps."

You wouldn't last ten minutes in the Corps, Striker thought to himself as he moved to stand at the head of the table. "FYI, several books have been written about the links between Marine Corps philosophy and successful business management."

"So you're going to treat us as if we were in boot camp?" Charles said, his voice mocking.

"An excellent idea." Striker's voice changed to that of a leader giving an order. "Hit the deck and give me twenty push-ups."

Charles blinked at him uncertainly. "You're kidding, right?"

"About the push-ups, yes. For now. But not about boot camp management."

"That's not realistic. The management of King Oil is a very complex issue, not something you can walk in off the street and comprehend."

"Unless you're a Marine."

"Again, no offense intended," Charles said in that condescending voice again, "but being a Marine doesn't give you superhuman abilities."

"It might. It definitely gives me the experience of dealing with complex situations. Successfully undertaking multiple missions. Handling a flood of raw information, or conversely a shortage of information. These things are our specialty. Marines thrive on multiple threats, situational ambiguity and rapidly changing conditions. What's the matter, Charles? You appear to be surprised by my comments. You didn't think a grunt from the Marines knew big words like *situational ambiguity?*"

Charles looked ready to swallow his tongue.

Striker looked around the room, his narrow gaze a challenge. "Anyone else care to comment? No? All right then. Another thing Marines are good at is taking complex issues and breaking them down to their essence. So tell me, what is the purpose of King Oil?"

He was greeted with dead silence.

"Come on, people," Striker said. "Give me some answers here."

"To make money," Charles stated.

"What else?" Striker said.

"To discover, manage and utilize our oil resources."

"What else?" Striker repeated.

"To be the best at what we do." This response came from a woman toward the back of the room.

"And how do we go about accomplishing those things?"

Again silence.

Striker sighed. "Let me tell you a little about the Marine Corps Officer Candidate School training. They don't just read a bunch of books or sit around and listen to lectures. They do that in addition to being herded from ten-mile marches to grueling calisthenics to crawls through the mud—without much sleep. Now I don't plan

on having you do all that. Not literally. But I want you
to think outside the box. I expect you to know what goes
on in this company, to be able to put yourselves in your
workers' shoes. I want fresh answers to old questions. I
want to see what kind of team you have going here.
What is this company's goal?''

"To make money," Charles repeated.

"I thought that was one of our purposes," Striker
countered.

"That can't be a goal and a purpose?"

"You tell me."

And so it went, with a majority of the old guard re-
maining stubbornly silent in their disapproval of such
goings-on.

But some of the younger members spoke up, brain-
storming ideas with relish as to creative ways of making
this company work without any further layoffs.

All the while, Striker stood back and observed how
the old guard continually shot down each new idea.

"We've never done things that way before," was a
mantra to them.

By the end of the day, Striker was ready to blow
something up. Seeing the top dogs' intractable insistence
on hanging on to the old way of doing business, Striker
was even more determined to speak to the rank-and-file
members of the company to get their input on things.
One idea that had come up today was instituting an em-
ployee suggestion box program, one that would be more
than just lip service.

Striker checked with Tex to schedule a meeting with
low-level managers and then arranged for visits to King
Oil's offshore oil rigs the following week.

"I heard you got a skunk by the tail," Tex told him.

"Is that your colorful Texas way of saying I stirred
things up at the meeting this afternoon?"

Tex nodded.

"Then yes, Tex, I reckon I do have a skunk by the tail," Striker drawled. "It sure stinks like a skunk and walks like a skunk."

"Well, you'd best get ready for more skunk chasing."

"And why's that?"

"Because the Oilman's Club is throwing a Texas barbecue in your honor this Saturday."

"Send my regrets," Striker said.

"I'll do that the day after a rooster lays an egg."

It took him a moment to translate that into a *no*. "Look, it just doesn't feel right given my grandfather's recent death to be out celebrating at a barbecue."

Tex laid her hand on his shoulder. "It's what Hank would have wanted."

Her comment irritated Striker instead of consoling him as she'd no doubt intended. "Do you think that's how I make my decisions, by doing what my grandfather would have wanted?"

"I think you could teach the folks around here a thing or two," she admitted. "If you don't blow them up first. Not that a few couldn't use a good demolition job."

Striker had to smile. "You know what? You'd make a fine Marine, Tex."

"And you'll make a fine Texan someday," Tex replied. "With enough coaching from me."

Chapter Five

Kate waited until Monday to drop by King Oil and check in with Striker. She wasn't avoiding him. She did have other cases that demanded her attention. But it was hard to focus on them, just as it was hard for her to sleep at night.

All because of that kiss. That one clear-off-the-Richter-scale kiss.

That was the reason she'd spent the past few nights tossing and turning in her bed, ending up with the luxurious 400-thread-count Italian damask top sheet wrapped around her body. It had taken her five minutes to untangle herself. Untangling her thoughts had been impossible.

And then there were the dreams. Not one but a series of them. All about Striker. She'd wake up and force herself to sit up and read an article from the latest issue of the *Texas Bar Journal*. Then she'd turn off the light again and fall asleep, only to pick up her erotic dream right where she'd left off—with Striker kissing her, his hands traveling over her body, exploring her with his fingertips, with his tongue, leaving no inch of her bare tingling skin untouched.

So here she was. Entering King Oil's headquarters. Wearing a burgundy suit by one of her favorite designers to give her confidence. *Not* to get Striker's attention. She didn't want or need that.

Her game plan was to remain calm and professional in order to hide the fact that she was rattled. That shouldn't be a problem. After all, Kate had been concealing her innermost emotions in one way or another for so many years now that this should be nothing new for her.

But, oh, this *was* new. Totally unchartered territory. And all because it involved one sexy, danger-loving Marine.

Not her forte, at all.

No, Kate's strength lay in keeping things under control, in following the rules and doing what was expected of her. And she was expected to make sure that this transition period between Striker and King Oil went smoothly. So here she was, doing her job.

Tex greeted Kate as she approached the company's inner sanctum. "You're looking a little better today."

"Is Striker in?" Kate asked.

Tex nodded.

"Is he still using that small conference room instead of Hank's old office?"

Tex nodded again.

"Okay if I go on in?"

"You tell me," Tex countered. "Will you be okay?"

The older woman's question caught Kate off guard. "Of course I'll be okay," she automatically replied. "Why wouldn't I be?"

"I don't know. Maybe because you lit out of here the

other day as if you were on fire. I tried talking to Striker about it, but he sidestepped me and shut up like a morning glory in the afternoon.''

Kate had to smile at the outrageous idea of likening Striker to a flower of any kind.

''Okay, so the man doesn't really resemble a morning glory,'' Tex admitted, ''but you know what I mean.''

''Occasionally Striker and I have a difference of opinion about various matters,'' Kate said. ''But that's all it is.''

Tex's expression was clearly disbelieving but she didn't press Kate any further, for which she was grateful.

After Tex's interrogation Kate escaped into the ladies' room, needing to make one final check to reassure herself that her makeup was perfect and that her expression showed none of her inner turmoil.

The outfit she wore was a power suit intended to make her feel invincible. A quick comb of her hair returned any wayward strands to obedient smoothness. And a dab of lipstick freshened her look.

Studying her reflection, Kate decided that she didn't look like a woman hiding secrets, like a woman at war with her own heart.

Too bad her outward appearance couldn't change her inner reality. But it did boost her confidence…being able to maintain the facade.

Even so, Kate's heart took a little leap when she entered the small conference room and first saw Striker, wearing jeans and a denim shirt as he had the other day. She vividly recalled the feel of the material beneath her fingertips.

She slammed the door on that train of thought and pretended to have her act together as she quietly closed the conference room door behind her.

"Hello, Striker." She sounded calm, which was a good thing. "How did your first week on the job go?"

"I survived it. I'm not sure the executives will ever be the same."

Kate didn't think she'd ever be the same, either, not after their kiss.

Objection. Illegal thought.

Sustained, her inner judge decreed.

"So you just dropped by to see how I was doing?" Striker asked. "Checking up on me?"

Kate didn't appreciate his suspicious tone. "No, that's not the reason for my visit. I have a few papers for you to sign regarding the estate."

When she handed them over to him, she noticed how he read every single word before signing his name at the bottom.

"You're not a man who trusts easily, are you?" she said.

"I'm a Force Recon Marine," Striker replied. "My survival depends on being constantly on guard for the worst."

In a strange sort of way, Kate knew how that felt. Because she was accustomed to being prepared for the worst as well. She was also accustomed to being prepared to do everything she could to maintain the status quo, to avoid disasters.

Not that a man like Striker would understand that. He didn't avoid trouble; he embraced it wholeheartedly.

Yet they both shared a similar guarded approach to certain situations. Kate didn't trust easily, either.

Having something in common with Striker did not make her feel better about things. Quite the opposite.

"What, you don't approve?" Striker asked her.

Kate blinked. "Excuse me?"

"You were giving me one of your looks," he said.

"What are you talking about?"

"One of your bug-under-a-microscope looks."

She wrinkled her nose. "That sounds real appealing."

"I wasn't trying to sweet-talk you."

"Good, because I wasn't looking to be sweet-talked," Kate retorted.

"If I were trying to sweet-talk you, you'd know it," Striker continued. "I'd say something about your incredible eyes…maybe that looking into them is like falling into the sky."

His voice had turned husky, seducing her with his intimate inflection. She'd never heard him speak this way before. Barking orders, expressing disapproval, these were things she was used to. Not seduction.

She almost leaned closer, before catching herself.

"That's what I'd say if I were trying to sweet-talk you," Striker said in his normal voice. "Probably something even better, but I'm kind of distracted this afternoon."

"Why's that?" Had he been distracted by the memory of their kiss the way she had?

"It's those idiot executives. And now I hear that even more idiot executives are organizing a barbecue for me this coming Saturday."

"What are you talking about? What idiots?"

"The Oilman's Club. They're organizing a barbecue to welcome me to San Antonio. I told Tex to tell them I wasn't coming."

"What did she say?"

"Something to do with a rooster, but the bottom line was that she disobeyed my order."

"How dare she," Kate noted dryly. "Disobey an order from you? Of all the nerve! What are you going to do? Are you going to have her court-martialed?"

Kate was actually teasing him. Striker found he liked

it. And he liked the way Kate looked all classy and un-touchable when he knew that she could be tousled with passion, her lips swollen from his kisses, her sky-blue eyes hazy with desire.

What had they been talking about? Oh, yeah. Tex. "I'll overlook her insubordination this time."

"I'm relieved to hear that."

"So back to this barbecue thing." He studied Kate closely. She looked so darn perfect, not a hair out of place. Which just made him want to reach out and be the one to mess her up, give her that sexy just-kissed look she had before. "Are you going to be there?"

She nodded.

"Good. I'll pick you up at six."

"Hold on a minute. I never said I'd go with you."

"Consider it part of your duties."

"Holding your hand while attending a barbecue is not in the job description."

"You have something against holding my hand?" Striker held it out for her to observe. "What's wrong? Too many calluses on it for a dainty, rich girl like you?"

"Listen, it's not my fault some rich girl dumped you at some point in your life. Get over it!"

"No rich girl dumped me." He was highly offended that she'd hit the nail on the head.

"No? Then where did this attitude of yours come from?"

"I've seen your type before."

"And what type would that be?"

"The rich, spoiled type."

"I am not spoiled. Far from it."

"Did you know that the executives here got a huge bonus last year paid for by laying off hundreds of work-ers?"

His seeming non sequitur appeared to throw her. "No, I didn't know that."

"Well, they did."

"And you somehow hold me responsible for that?"

Striker knew he was being unreasonable and that irked him. He normally prided himself on his logical approach to problems. Sure, there were times when his hotshot ways had gotten him into trouble, but more times than not they'd saved a mission.

Dealing with Kate wasn't like dealing with a mission, however. He couldn't figure her out. Was she still mourning the death of a fiancé who had died a decade ago? Had she loved the guy that much? Striker wanted to ask her these questions, but he didn't know how.

So he got mad. Not smart. Not productive. But there you had it. He wasn't working on home territory here.

Striker could cope with jungles or desert terrain. He could scale a rock face, could survive for days in the harshest jungles with nothing more than a KA-BAR knife in his kit. But he couldn't figure out this woman. What made her tick. What made her special. What made her smile.

Maybe if he spent more time with her, he'd figure the puzzle out and be able to move on. Yes, that sounded logical.

Striker felt better having a plan, and that one sounded as good as any.

Spending more time with her meant convincing her to come to this stupid welcome party thing with him. Being a bottom-line kind of guy, he used that approach. "If you don't go with me, I'll blow off this barbecue."

"You can't do that. It's being held in your honor. The members of the Oilman's Club would be horribly offended."

"Do I look like I care?" he countered.

"What *do* you care about?" she surprised him by asking.

"The Marine Corps and my family."

"In that order?"

He didn't answer.

"So your career comes before your family? Well, that's something you should have in common with those executives."

"I'm nothing like them!" His anger was clear.

"Prove it," she challenged him.

"I don't have to prove it. I don't have to prove anything."

"Neither do I," Kate retorted. "I don't have to prove I'm not a spoiled rich girl. You should be judging me by my actions and not your preconceived prejudices."

Her vehement words caught him by surprise. She had him there. He had been judging her based on his prior experiences with ritzy females, not by her own actions. Sure, she'd been a bit bossy. And yes she'd had an Ice Queen demeanor at times. But now he knew why. Nothing she'd done was all that bad. "You're right," he said slowly.

"Wh-what?" she stuttered.

"I said you're right. You don't have to look so shocked. I am willing to admit when I'm wrong. It doesn't happen very often, but it does happen on rare occasions. When it does, I'm man enough to own up to it."

Oh, Striker was man enough, all right. All six-foot-whatever of him. With his dark hair and green eyes. She'd never been that fond of green eyes before. But his were special. They held secrets, they revealed flashes of the man beneath.

These were dangerous waters, here. She needed to

keep her distance, not become even more intrigued by him.

"It's just a Texas barbecue," she said. "You don't need me."

"What if I said I do need you?"

His voice had gone all husky again, making her heart do somersaults.

What would it be like to be needed by a man like him? Would it make him as vulnerable as she was? She had a hard time imagining him as anything other than in charge. She could see him wanting her, knew he'd wanted her when he'd kissed her the other day. But *need?* That was something else. A different level.

And then there was love. Yet another level.

What would it be like to be loved by a man like Striker? To be both needed and desired, to be cherished and seduced, to both have power and be powerless?

If things were different…if she were different, if he weren't a man addicted to danger…

Ah, but it was tempting to wonder what if…

Tempting but pointless. Yet there was no denying the powerful hold he had on her. Maybe *hold* was too strong a word. Maybe not.

Kate only knew that the teenage fantasy crush she'd harbored for Striker was rapidly growing into something else and she didn't seem to be able to do anything about it.

"What would I do if you said you needed me?" she belatedly repeated his question. "Men like you don't need anyone else."

"If I say I won't use the phrase *women like you,* will you agree not to use the phrase *men like you?* Let's try working with a new concept here. That we are not like anyone we've ever met before. Start with a fresh slate. What do you say?" Striker held out his hand. "Deal?"

The prospect of starting anew was incredibly tantalizing. Her usual cautious self warned her not to let down her guard, but in the end she couldn't resist his offer. "Deal."

Kate shook his hand, trying desperately to pretend he was just another client. That didn't stop the inner shivers from racing through her body, making her nerve endings hum with awareness of the texture of his skin, the strength of his lean fingers, the brush of his thumb against the back of her hand.

"And you'll come with me to this stupid barbecue?" he asked.

What was that saying—in for a penny, in for a pound? "All right. I'll come with you. But all you have to do is show up and be charming," she said. "Nothing can go wrong."

"Don't say that," Striker warned her. "Being convinced that nothing can go wrong is an invitation for *everything* to go wrong."

"How do I look?" Striker asked Tony before muttering, "I can't believe I'm asking this of a guy who wears big fat bunny slippers."

Striker had never cared how he looked before. Not that he didn't take pride in his appearance. A Marine was taught to do so the moment he entered boot camp. Taking care of his uniform was a part of his military training.

On those rare occasions when Striker was off duty, he preferred hanging out at his beach house on a tiny coastal island off of North Carolina wearing only khaki shorts and one of his colorful Hawaiian shirts.

Texas, however, was not Hawaiian-shirt territory. This here was denim territory.

So Striker was wearing jeans and a freshly pressed

denim cowboy shirt complete with white pearlized snaps down the front and on the pockets. The worn brown leather belt with a silver buckle and brown leather cowboy boots lacked the glitz of an urban cowboy, and instead reflected the fact that he'd owned them for some time.

The black Stetson was a new addition. There was nothing fancy about it, but it felt a little strange wearing it instead of his Marine Corps cover. He prayed he didn't look like a total idiot.

"You look nervous, Striker." Tony's wide smile was clearly mocking. "Why is that?"

"I do not look nervous. You just can't see very well," he retorted. "Consuela told me that you need glasses but won't wear them."

"She should not be gossiping," Tony grumbled.

"Hey, you're the one who started it by telling her about Kate sleeping here."

"I told you, Consuela saw the unmade bed."

Striker waved the older man's words away. "You could have made up a story." Luckily Consuela had the day off and couldn't hear them.

"I am not as good at espionage as you."

"I'm a Force Recon Marine, not James Bond." Although when he added the aviator sunglasses he often wore, Striker decided he did look like a new kind of cowboy/Marine hybrid.

"Kate is pulling up now," Tony noted with a nod at the window in the large living room that looked out on the front of the house.

Striker checked his watch. She was right on time. Good. He liked that in a woman. In his experience they often lacked any concept of time. To them five minutes meant half an hour or more. But not to Kate.

He opened the door to find her standing there, looking

more casual today than he'd ever seen her. A brown skirt swirled around her ankles, displaying her fancy hand-tooled boots.

He'd have preferred seeing her in something short, like cut-offs and a halter top.

Hey, a guy could dream, couldn't he?

The problem was that he was still dreaming about Kate at night. He couldn't get the memory of their kiss out of his mind.

She was wearing a white shirt with some kind of horse print on it in brown and black outlines. The shirt was unbuttoned, displaying the matching top beneath it. The scooped neckline showed him just a hint of her cleavage, leaving him wanting more.

Yeah, Kate was real good at that. Leaving him wanting more.

She had her hair down loose, falling around her shoulders. This way he could appreciate its golden color even more. Certain strands were lighter than others, making him want to reach out and touch them.

"You look great," he murmured, removing his sunglasses to get a better look at her.

"Thanks. So do you."

"So I pass inspection?"

Kate nodded. Striker more than just passed, he took her breath away. He didn't possess the kind of sex appeal that knocked you over the head, it kind of snuck up on you. He had an easy way of moving, powerful and confident but not in your face.

And then there were his eyes. Mirrors to the soul. But Striker wasn't a man to bare his soul to anyone. But just because he disguised his emotions didn't mean that he didn't possess them. She'd met plenty of men who were so self-involved that they had no depth. That wasn't the case with Striker. He ran very deep, like a vein of gold deep in the earth.

"I should have picked you up," Striker was saying.

"I live in the middle of the city. Nowhere near where we're going."

"So what? You don't trust my driving?"

She didn't trust herself. She could already feel her backbone melting and she'd just arrived. The idea of him coming into her home, her one final sanctuary, was just too much. So she made excuses, valid ones. "I was out this way visiting my parents anyway."

"And you didn't want me picking you up over there because…?"

"I wanted to save you from the interrogation my mother gives everyone who goes out with me. Not that you're really going out with me," she quickly clarified. "This is a business thing. My father understands that."

"Won't your parents be there today?" he asked.

"They had to decline because of a previous engagement."

"Wish I'd done that," Striker muttered.

"He's nervous," Tony told Kate, entering the conversation.

"Not true," Striker denied.

"Striker nervous? I find that hard to believe, Tony," Kate said.

"I am telling you it is so," Tony said.

"The man wears bunny slippers. You can't trust a word he says," Striker retorted. "Come on." He reached out to cup her elbow in his hand. "Let's go."

"Just wait until you have grandchildren," Tony called after him. "Then we will see who laughs last."

"His grandkids got him the slippers," Striker explained at Kate's frown of confusion.

"Can you see yourself having kids?" Kate heard herself asking Striker before she could stop herself.

He shrugged. "Maybe. Someday. How about you?"

"Maybe. Someday." She repeated his words. "Yes, I could definitely see myself having kids. You know, when I was in law school I wanted to go into public law, maybe working in Children's Services as an advocate for kids and families in need."

"So what stopped you?"

Duty. Duty stopped her. And fear. Not that she'd tell him that. "I followed in my father's footsteps like you did. Your father was a Marine right?"

"Right. He's retired now."

"I've been meaning to ask you if you've been in touch with your mother? Please feel free to give her my name and phone number if she has any questions or anything."

Right. Like that was going to happen. His mom talking to Kate was the last thing Striker needed right now.

His mom had a way of ferreting out his secrets and the possibility that she might cotton on to the notion that Striker was attracted to Kate would not be a good thing.

No, his mother and Kate speaking to one another was definitely something to be avoided.

"Yes, I've talked to my mother since I got here. There's no need for you to speak to her."

"How is she taking Hank's death?" Kate's voice reflected her concern.

"My mom's a strong woman. She copes."

Kate couldn't help wondering if Striker's mom *really* coped or was just good at conning others the way that Kate was. Kate had never met her but had heard stories about her—disapproving tales from Hank and fond ones from Kate's father who had grown up with Angela King before she became Angela Kozlowski.

"My dad knew your mom before she married your father, you know," Kate said. "I guess they sort of grew up together, with her being the girl-next-door and all."

This came as news to Striker. His mom rarely talked about her growing-up years. When she did, it was usually some funny story about shaking scorpions out of her boots or something. Apparently the venomous devils had no respect for wealth or power. They crawled wherever they wanted.

But she didn't talk about her father, other than to say the obvious. That he was a headstrong stubborn man used to having his own way.

Death had a way of making you realize that life isn't open-ended. It wasn't a realization Striker relished. He didn't want to think about death, he wanted to focus on living.

Sure he got a rush out of flirting with danger, and yes that made him feel more alive. But he never really considered the possibility that he wouldn't make it back from a mission. What was the point in doing that?

No, he'd much rather spend his time living in the moment. Which was why he bent closer to inhale Kate's tempting perfume.

"You smell good," he murmured.

There it was again, that seducing voice he'd used the other day when he'd pretended to be sweet-talking her. He had only to speak a few words and she was ready to melt.

If only he were different. If only she were different, able to handle his need for speed, his love for his work as a Force Recon Marine, living on the edge.

The problem with loving someone who lived on the edge was that you could be in for a terrible fall.

That didn't scare some people. But Kate was different. She'd been burned, more than once. She'd tried several times to boldly go after what she wanted. But each time something bad had happened.

The first time she'd been just a child. Her seventh birthday. Kate hadn't wanted to go to visit her grandmother in Dallas. She'd wanted to stay home and have a party instead. She'd cried, and had eventually gotten her way. Kate hadn't visited her grandmother. Three days later, Grandma Alicia died of a stroke.

Then there was Ted. She'd secretly wanted out of their engagement. Ted died.

She'd wanted out of the family law firm and her father had suffered a near-fatal heart attack.

So call her a wimp, call her superstitious.

But the bottom line was that when Kate tried to go after what she wanted, people died or got hurt.

But, oh, Striker made her want to forget all that. He made her want to take risks.

And so here she was, going with him to the barbecue even though he was perfectly capable of managing without her help.

Just as she had to be perfectly capable of enjoying her time with Striker without making a big deal out of it.

The fact that it was a beautiful day helped keep her mind off darker thoughts. Although it was mid-September, the temperatures were more in keeping with mid-July. Temperatures were already in the low nineties and thunderstorms were predicted for later in the day. But for now, the big Texas sky was populated with only a handful of cumulous clouds, looking like dollops of whipped cream placed in a Wedgwood blue bowl.

Striker, apparently, was not equally appreciative of Mother Nature's work. Instead he was fixing her lemon-yellow VW Beetle with a dismissive look.

"I hope you didn't plan on us going in your little car."

"I hadn't thought about it." But visions of him stashed beside her in the close confines of her cute car were getting her hot and bothered.

"I expected to see you driving some fancy imported convertible."

"It's in the shop." That was true. The Mercedes her father had given her for her last birthday was waiting for a back-ordered part. Not that Striker had actually ever seen her car. It irked her that his mocking lucky guess had been an accurate one. She'd bought the VW for herself. The Mercedes was for show, the VW was her workhorse.

"We'll go in the truck." Striker had commandeered one of the ranch's pickups, a bright red Ford. He held the passenger door open for her and offered her his free hand to assist her in getting in.

Striker noticed the ruffled hint of the white petticoat peeking from beneath her skirt. Maybe there was something to be said for long skirts after all, he decided, appreciating the flash of bare skin on her calf as she hopped up onto the running board and slid into the seat.

Yeah, there was definitely something about viewing forbidden hidden territory to having everything on display.

Who knew? Who knew he'd be turned on by the flip of a long skirt blowing in the breeze, or by the view of fancy lace on a petticoat? He'd never thought of himself as an old-fashioned kind of guy before. But then Kate had a way of bringing out new depths within him.

Walking around the front of the truck, Striker slid his sunglasses into place and watched her through the windshield. She still looked regal, even wearing supposedly casual clothes.

When they arrived at the barbecue, he understood why.

This was no redneck celebration—this was fancy fare. Regal stuff. Not that you could tell from the entrance. That was typical of any Texas ranch, including his grandfather's Westwind. A carved wood sign hung over the cattle guard and a long one-laned drive lined with mesquite trees led to the ranch house. But the similarities ended there.

First off, there was valet parking by guys wearing fancy little red vests over white shirts and black pants. Then there was the house. It was huge, even by Texas standards.

There were three levels, complete with scrollwork balconies and huge windows, built into a rolling hillside. The place was the size of an aircraft carrier.

The back patio was big enough to land a Marine Corps Super Stallion helo. Fancy flowers and plants in huge Mexican clay pots were strewn around the perimeter. Hand-tooled leather equipage chairs and matching tables were placed in groups.

And then there was the food. The selections on the buffet table had scrolled handwritten descriptions— smoked quail and lobster nachos, sour-mango coleslaw, grilled corn with chili-basil butter, chipotle-and-braised-mushroom enchiladas with salsa verde. All looked over by more serving staff.

Over in the grilling area there was a heaping pile of ribs and chicken. The smell of mesquite wood and barbecue sauce made his mouth water.

"Looks better than an M.R.E.," Striker said.

"What's that?"

"Meals ready to eat. Combat food. In packets. Trust me, it's not devised with taste in mind."

Striker's words reminded Kate that he was more Marine than cowboy, despite the black Stetson he was wearing so well.

"You know, I'll bet that that's probably what the Patterson's told their caterer. We want a spread that looks better than an M.R.E." Teasing him somehow made things easier to manage. Kate had discovered that for the first time the other day when she'd teased him about court-martialing Tex.

Striker grinned and her heart leapt. "Yeah, well they did a good job."

"Welcome, you two," their host William "Bubba" Patterson said in his booming voice. "Welcome to my humble home. *Mi casa, es su casa.*"

Striker couldn't help wondering how many workers this guy had laid off to manage this kind of mansion. The thought brought home how different he was from all these other people, including Kate. She fit in here. He didn't.

Striker wasn't part of their world. He was a fish out of water. Not that anyone else would be able to tell that. When he wanted to, Striker could blend in to any situation. That was a requirement of his special forces training. There were times when standing out could get you killed.

"It was kind of you to throw this party to welcome Striker to Texas," Kate said on his behalf.

Striker wasn't real fond of people talking for him, but he tried to rein in his irritation.

"No problem," Bubba replied. "I was real fond of your granddaddy, Striker. He was a fine Texan."

Striker didn't know what to say to that, so he just nodded.

"Well, enough shooting the breeze," Bubba declared. "Go on and grab some grub. We've got music starting later. Give you both a chance to practice your Texas two-step."

"Why the frown?" Kate asked Striker after Bubba had moved on to greet others. "Don't you dance?"

"I manage." Striker hadn't been real fond of dancing for years after that country club debacle on his nineteenth birthday, with his grandfather trying to force Striker's hand by announcing in front of everyone that Striker was joining King Oil and not the Marines. But then a little cutie named Zoe in a honky-tonk out in San Diego had shown him the fun to be had by kicking up your heels.

"Why were you frowning then?" Kate asked.

"Marines don't frown. We show no facial expression other than our battle face. We do eat lawyers who keep us from food, however. So let's go eat."

This time Striker took her hand instead of her elbow. The feel of his fingers linked with hers created an all-too-familiar buzz that zipped throughout her body. He had strong hands, with lean fingers. There was a newfound sense of recognition within her, as if the missing piece of a puzzle had just fallen into place. Her hand did fit into his that way, as if meant to mesh together smoothly.

When they arrived at the buffet table, he released her to hand her a plate. The sense of loss was so strong that it pierced right through her defenses and made a direct hit on her heart.

If she felt this way after less than two weeks in his company, how would she feel when he left after two months?

What if Striker didn't leave? What if the Marine Corps ordered him to stay?

She closed her eyes for a moment, imagining what it would be like…having him in her life permanently. Having this traveling Marine settle down, marrying, having kids. All with her.

"Do you want more?" Striker asked.

Her eyes flew open. "More?" Her voice was husky. No, she wouldn't want more than that...having him safe by her side would be a dream come true.

But dreams didn't come true. Not for her. Instead they tended to turn into nightmares.

Chapter Six

Striker decided that he just wasn't a sour-mango cole-slaw kind of guy. But the ribs…ah now, those were some of the best he'd ever eaten. The tender meat fell off the bone and the barbecue sauce might just be as good as his mom's. And all of this washed down with a cold bottle of Mexican beer.

Yeah, the food was great. But Kate had gone quiet since they'd stood at the buffet table and gotten their fancy china plates, the ones with the silhouette of bucking cowboys painted around the edges. No paper plates for this crowd.

The way Kate was daintily nibbling on the ribs made his mouth water. He wanted to taste her, wanted to lick the tangy sauce from her lips. And then he wanted to lick his way down to the hollow of her throat, before going lower still to the shadowy valley between her breasts. It was so hot that she'd removed her overshirt and was just wearing the sleeveless top that matched it.

But his thoughts weren't consumed with her clothes.

They were consumed with what she'd look like *without* them.

Striker remembered the feel of her silky thighs when he'd removed her stockings that first night. And the feel of her breasts against the backs of his fingers as he'd undone her suit jacket.

She hadn't been wearing any jewelry that night. Today she was wearing a dainty necklace of liquid silver and turquoise that nestled in the hollow of her throat. The other women at the barbecue all wore big chunks of diamonds. But not Kate.

With her, less was more.

Was that why she got to him so badly?

Striker reminded himself that he had a plan here. Spend more time with her, get to know her better, figure out why she got under his skin.

Well, he was doing that, and so far no lightbulb had gone on over his head answering all his questions. There had been no "aha" moment; no "this is the secret" revelations. He hadn't cracked the code yet.

Because she was distracting him, licking her lips that way. Making him all hot.

While no expert on social niceties, Striker was pretty sure that yanking her into his arms and having his wicked way with her right here in the middle of the crowded patio would probably be frowned upon.

So why was she so quiet? Had she guessed that he was sitting here imagining making love to her? Hot, passionate, sweaty love—the kind that made you howl at the moon. Had she felt that way about the guy she was engaged to?

The possibility made him feel strange inside. A little like a raw recruit charging up a hill wearing fifty pounds of combat gear…combined with the twist in his gut resulting from that time he'd leapt off what seemed like a thousand-foot-high waterfall on a special op in the jungles of the Philippines. Was this what jealousy felt like? Raw, on the verge of gut-wrenching?

No way. He'd never been the jealous type. Never one to get too involved.

Footloose and fancy free, that his was modus operandi. He'd seen his buddies Justice Wilder and Justice's youngest brother, Sam, fall victim to Cupid's arrows. And, yeah, okay, so things had worked out fine for them and for their other brothers. All the Wilder boys were married now. Apparently, happily so.

He was glad for them. But marriage... No, that wasn't for him. Striker valued his freedom. Sure he'd settle down someday. But not now. He wasn't ready.

He glanced over at Kate. She'd finally finished nibbling on the rib and was dabbing at her lips with one corner of the oversized red gingham napkin they'd all been given. Despite her best efforts, she'd missed a spot of barbecue sauce on her chin.

He almost leaned over and kissed it off. But he stopped himself at the last moment.

Now he was so close to her he could see her eyes widen. Could see little wisps of her hair shimmering around her face.

"Is something wrong?" Kate almost didn't recognize her own voice, so husky was it. She hadn't expected Striker to lean forward as if he were about to consume her with one of his awesome kisses again. Because they'd both agreed that kissing wasn't a good idea. Right?

She'd felt him looking at her while they sat at a table for two, ignoring the crowd around them. Some part of her realized that since Striker was the guest of honor, they really should have chosen one of the larger tables and been more sociable. But instead they'd gravitated to a quieter corner of the patio.

"Affirmative," Striker belatedly replied, using his seducing voice.

"Affirmative?" She blinked.

"Affirmative, something is wrong."

"What is it?"

"Don't look so worried. It's nothing earth-shattering. You've just got some barbecue sauce right here." Instead of using his napkin, or even her own, he gently swiped her chin with the tip of his thumb. The brush of his work-roughened skin against her generated a waterfall of delicious pleasure.

Keeping his intense green eyes fixed on hers, he shifted his thumb from her chin directly to his own mouth, "Mmm, very tasty."

She'd seen those scenes in movies where the guy did something like Striker had just done and her girlfriends had all gone "Ohhhh." She'd never gotten it. Never understood. Now she did.

He was tasting *her.*

What an incredibly arousing surprise this was. The crowd around them faded away as she kept her gaze on his eyes. It was as if she couldn't look away. As if they were in a visual lock, reminding her of their mind-blowing lip-lock of a kiss.

She loved his eyes. They were infinitely green. Not grass-green, not bottle-green. Sometimes they were shadowy green, filled with hidden emotions. Not now. Now they reflected heated passion, telling her without speaking that he wanted her.

"There you two are, hiding way over here." Bubba's booming voice broke the spell. "So how are you enjoying yourself so far, Striker?"

"It's been a real…pleasure," Striker replied, keeping his gaze on Kate a moment longer.

"Glad to hear that you're appreciating our Texas hospitality."

"Once you've had a taste, it's real hard to resist."

Kate knew Striker wasn't talking about hospitality.

But Bubba just slapped Striker on the back and laughed heartily. "Before we begin the dancing, I wanted to introduce you to a few folks."

Bubba whisked Striker away. Well, not exactly whisked. There was no whisking a six-foot-something, lean-mean-fighting Marine. Striker did go with Bubba, but not before giving Kate a meaningful look along with the husky promise, "I'll be back."

Kate barely had time to cool herself down with a sip of iced tea before the first in a long series of women dropped into the empty seat and grilled her. Each one had a different question. "So what's the deal with you two? Are you seeing him? What do your parents think about him? If you're not seeing him, will you give him my phone number?"

That last question elicited a frown and the closest thing to a glare that a cultured woman like Kate possessed. She was about to say, "Give him your phone number yourself," before realizing that this woman would do just that.

So what? Why should she care? She and Striker weren't seeing each other.

Liar. That look they'd shared before he'd left had been intimate enough to make her insides melt. There was plenty of *seeing* going on.

They weren't dating. He was just a business associate. Who happened to drive her crazy with desire.

Not that she shared that last tidbit with the women who flocked to her table, eager for some tidbit about the latest hottie to join their ranks. He was fresh meat, and they were eager for a taste.

Taste…that brought her thoughts back to him swiping the sauce from her chin and licking it from his thumb.

Even the memory was powerful enough to make her go all weak and hot in those places a decent woman wasn't supposed to talk about. At least not at a public gathering like this.

Not that the other women were showing equal restraint. They were extremely free in their discussion of Striker and his attributes.

"Did you see that butt of his? Primo stuff," Veronica Sands bluntly declared, waggling her manicured fingers in his direction. She was the trophy wife of an oilman forty years her senior. "Don't tell me you haven't noticed? I find that hard to believe."

"We're business associates." Kate took another sip of iced tea, refusing to give in to the urge to toss it at Veronica.

"Yes, I know. Business associates. You told me that already." Veronica kept her avid gaze on Striker. "That doesn't mean you can't admire a great butt when you see one. And a mighty nice set of shoulders, too. Wide, narrow waist, trim butt. Oh, yes. Good in bed, for sure. I do believe I'll mosey on over there and have Bubba introduce me." Veronica was practically licking her lips.

"Have Bubba introduce your husband to Striker as well," Kate said.

Veronica just laughed. "As if. My husband is inside talking business with a bunch of old cronies. No, Striker and I can manage quite well on our own."

Maybe they could. Veronica was a gorgeous woman. With a gorgeous body. Of course, much of it was thanks to her plastic surgeon. But some guys weren't so

choosey. They took one look at those breasts and they
didn't care if they were silicone implants.

Veronica made the most of them, as she was today,
wearing a halter top with a suede honey-colored skirt
that hung so low on her hips it was amazing that it didn't
fall off.

Maybe that was the kind of woman that Striker went
for. The obvious type.

Kate propped her chin in her hand, the same chin that
Striker had caressed, and watched Veronica move like a
shark after fresh meat through the crowd until she
reached Striker's side.

"Hey, there, Bubba, aren't you going to introduce me
to our guest of honor?"

Striker turned to find a woman by his side. A second
later she had her hands wrapped around his arm and was
leaning against him. From his vantage point he had an
unrestricted view of an impressive pair of breasts. Not
real, of course. And not as sexy as Kate's.

There was a time when a woman like this would have
gotten his engine going. But not now. Now a barely
there halter top showing off her considerable assets
didn't have a millionth of the effect of that fluttering
petticoat hem of Kate's showing a glimpse of her ankles
and calves.

Oh, yeah, this was proof that he had it bad. Whatever
it was. Sexual attraction. Yeah, he was comfortable with
that. He was sexually attracted to Kate. That's why this
woman left him cold.

Figuring it out should have made him feel better. But
it didn't. Because sexual attraction had never felt this
way before.

But he'd go with that diagnosis…for now.

Bubba obligingly made the introductions. "Striker,

meet Veronica Sands. Her husband, Jimmie Bob, is one of our charter members.''

Veronica flashed Striker a smile brighter than the boulder of a diamond on her left hand. ''If you need anyone to show you the ropes, Striker, feel free to call on me. Here, let me write down my private cell phone number for you.'' She pulled out a card and a solid-gold pen. She then propped the card on Striker's back and took her time writing the number.

Striker guessed from the reaction of their host that this was typical behavior for Veronica. When she finally finished writing, she handed the card to Striker, making sure to let her fingers linger on his. ''You be sure and give me a call, you hear? Now, Bubba, when is this dancin' you been promisin' us gonna start?''

Her hungry look in Striker's direction let him know that she was looking to start something more than just dancing.

''Excuse me, but I've got to get back to Kate,'' he said.

Veronica frowned, or at least gave her version of a frown. He suspected she'd had a few of those injections to ward off wrinkles because her face had a tight look to it. ''What's your hurry, big boy? She told me that you two are just business associates. In case you haven't heard, she's not exactly got a reputation for having fun.''

Striker's expression hardened as he removed Veronica's possessive hand from his arm and gave her a look that made those under his command wilt. Startled, Veronica took a step back. Without saying a word, Striker walked away.

Kate watched him come back to the table. Was he returning to tell her that he was going to go off with Veronica?

Where did that wild idea come from? she demanded

of the inner demon sitting on her proverbial shoulder. *Why do you always assume the worst?*

Because if you prepare for the worst, then you won't be disappointed if things don't work out. Sure, she ran through worst-case scenarios in the cases she worked on, but she wasn't aware that that philosophy had crept into her personal life.

Not that she had much of a personal life lately. Most of her time was devoted to her work.

By the time Striker joined her, the band had started playing. "Why did you sic that barracuda on me?" he demanded as he sat down across from her.

Whatever she'd expected him to say, it wasn't that.

"Are you referring to Veronica?" Kate said.

He nodded. "She's not my type."

"No?"

"No." He leaned forward and brushed his fingertips over the back of her hand. "I seem to have developed a fondness for fancy lady lawyers wearing petticoats. Come on." He threaded his fingers through hers and tugged her to her feet. "Let's dance."

He led her to join the others in a Texas two-step, his arm around her waist as they moved with the couples. The feel of his muscular body pressed so close to hers made dancing difficult. It made breathing difficult, too!

"You're thinking too much," he leaned down to whisper in her ear. "Just relax and feel. Feel the music…"

The beat was coming faster now, as they swirled around. There was no time for thinking, only for laughing and trying to keep up.

Striker realized that this was the first time he'd ever heard her laugh so much. He also realized that the sound of it made him want her even more. Her lips were parted, her cheeks flushed from exertion, her eyes bluer than he could find words to describe.

The next thing he knew, he'd stumbled over his own two feet. Pulling her closer, he avoided bumping into the couple near them. Now she was facing him, rather than tucked beside him. Her breasts were pressed against his chest. The thin material of her top and his shirt did little to disguise the fact that her nipples were standing at attention, their tips temptingly erect. She was breathing fast. He could barely breathe at all.

He swung her off the dance floor and toward the protection of a huge plant, taller and wider than he was. Her face was tilted up to his. She nervously licked her lips and he groaned, knowing he was a goner. Like a homing device guiding an aircraft in, his mouth homed in on hers.

But before his lips landed on hers, they were interrupted by the rowdy voices of a group of men who'd clearly enjoyed a few too many alcoholic beverages.

Striker tugged Kate out of their way as the group almost knocked over the planter with their pushing and shoving.

"Watch it, boys," he growled.

"Who are you callin' a boy?" one of them growled right back.

"You better speak slowly," another mocked. "He's got the look of an Aggie."

Kate hastily intervened in case Striker wasn't familiar with the term to describe someone who attended Texas A&M University.

"He's a Marine," Kate said. "Not an Aggie."

"Aggies are the enemy," the first one growled.

Through the open French doors, Kate caught a glimpse of the sixty-inch flat screen TV displaying a college football game. She wondered if the Aggies were playing the University of Texas. Those games were big deals in this part of the country. Any college football game was—high school, too, for that matter.

Football had never really appealed to her. Her father was a huge University of Texas fan, however, which was probably the so-called prior engagement he had that prevented him from coming to the barbecue today. She should have figured that out. Her dad had one entire room devoted to team memorabilia. It was near the garage area, away from the main part of the house at her mother's insistence. Elizabeth didn't want any of that tacky stuff clashing with her expensive decorating.

"A Marine?" the biggest of the group of rowdies slurred. He looked wide enough to be a defensive lineman on any football team. "Who do they play for?"

"The United States of America," Striker replied, clearly getting impatient with these bunch of yahoos.

Kate placed a soothing hand on his arm. All she needed was a fist fight here. "There was a football game. Texans tend to take their football pretty seriously. Plus there's a long rivalry between Aggies and the University of Texas."

Striker could understand rivalries. The army/navy football games had a long history as well. Marines played on the navy team.

The drunken group started singing some kind of college fight song. It was soon countered by a new group rapidly closing in, singing another song, presumably the University of Texas song.

Striker had been involved in enough fights to recognize the signs. Fists were going to start swinging any second. Not his problem. Getting Kate out of the way was his priority.

Keeping his arm around her, he efficiently whisked her away from the confrontation.

"Remember when you said nothing could go wrong and I told you not to say that?" Striker said once they reached the opposite side of the huge patio. "That it was an invitation for disaster?"

"This isn't a disaster. It's just a misunderstanding."

No sooner had Kate said those words than the hefty guy knocked over the huge potted plant, its long branches landing in the middle of the barbecue sauce, splattering it all over, before landing on the edge of the huge platter of ribs. Seconds later ribs rained down from skies darkening with storm clouds.

"*Now* it's a disaster," Kate decided.

"I'll say one thing," Striker drawled. "You Texans sure know how to throw a party."

Flashes of lightning accompanied them all the way home. Instead of the storm breaking, it just seemed to keep building along the western horizon. By the time they reached Westwind, Kate recognized the dangerous blue-black color of the sky. This was no mere storm. This was tornado weather.

Tony greeted them as they got out of the truck. "Twister's coming! Head for the storm cellar. I'm goin' to join the men." He pointed to the guys opening the cellar door in the ground near the barn.

There wasn't time for Striker to go with him. The light became eerie, pale around the edges but midnight dark at the core. The rolling mass was closing in fast from the southwest. No skinny twister here.

And now the wind, strong enough to bend the trees and break off branches. Much worse was to come.

Striker grabbed Kate's hand and ran to the cellar along the far side of the ranch house. Fighting the wind, he yanked the doors up and hurried her inside. She didn't seem eager to go.

The doors fell shut with a thump as he hurried down the cement steps. The area was dark, but his eyes quickly adjusted. He could see Kate's pale face.

"It'll be okay." He'd been in the cellar before, when he'd spent the summer there. Sure enough, the flashlight was still stored in the same place. He grabbed it and switched it on.

"Come here." He moved her away from the entrance and farther into the protection of the corner. The cellar was not huge. You weren't meant to stay in here for long. Just long enough to get out of the path of a twister or grab some of the supplies stored there.

The air was cool and a bit stale from being closed up. They were beneath ground level. The walls were lined with shelves. It looked like a number of them held Consuela's canned tomatoes. A simple pine bench rested against the back wall.

Sitting down, he gently pulled Kate onto his lap. "Are you afraid of tornadoes?"

"Anyone in their right mind would be afraid of them. They're powerful enough to take a building and move it right off its foundations. I heard about a case where it took a flag from a golf course and carried it forty-three miles away." Talking about statistics usually made her feel more in command. Not this time.

"We're safe here. No tornado is going to carry you anywhere."

"I don't like enclosed spaces." Her voice was unsteady, as were her fingers when they clenched his shoulders.

And then there came the sound. Like a bunch of freight trains. The sound of the twister approaching made conversation impossible. So Striker comforted her without words, with his touch.

Kate meant to bury her face in his shoulder but somehow she ended up brushing her lips against his cheek. Mother Nature roared her displeasure even as the blood rushed through Kate's body. Then his mouth covered hers, softly at first, testing her reaction.

The crash of something hitting the cellar door had Striker automatically putting himself between her and danger. The kiss was over and several seconds of mayhem followed, the roar of the storm, the pounding of hail, more crashes. Striker held her in his protective embrace, his strength a tangible thing.

Then there was silence followed by rain.

Kate removed her face from his shoulder. "Do you think the worst is over?"

He nodded. "Sounds that way."

"I need to get out." She couldn't breathe and it wasn't because of Striker's sex appeal. It was because of her claustrophobia.

"Okay. Take it easy. You'll be out in a minute."

But the door wouldn't open. Something had landed on top of it.

"Are we trapped?" Her voice was frantic.

"No," he reassured her. "Tony is out there. He'll get a few of the hands to clear away whatever it is that's blocking the door. No problem. It'll just take them a minute or two."

"What if they can't get to us? What if the house fell on the cellar door and we're under piles and piles of rubbish?"

"The house is too well built to fall down."

"Not if a twister hit it."

"You're hyperventilating." He rubbed a soothing hand on her back as he stood beside her. "Just calm down."

"I told you... I don't...like enclosed spaces."

"Fear's a funny thing."

His comment irritated her. Here she was gasping for breath and he reacts this way? "I fail to see any humor in the situation."

"I just meant that it's a strange thing. I've often found that fear can lead you to what you fear most."

"Meaning I was afraid of the storm, so it led me here, where I'm even more afraid? Not that fear is a concept you'd understand. Marines don't feel fear right?"

"They're stupid if they don't. The thing is not to let fear rule you. You've probably heard that phrase about courage not being lack of fear but the ability to over-come it." He smoothed a hand over her hair and cupped his palm over her soft cheek. "It's okay to be afraid, providing you don't let it immobilize you."

"What are you afraid of?"

"Sexy lady lawyers with eyes bluer than a Texas sky."

"You're sweet-talking me again."

"No, ma'am," he said solemnly. But in the limited light thrown out by the flashlight she could see a gleam of humor in his vivid green eyes. "I'd never do a thing like that."

"Why? Because you're afraid of lady lawyers?"

"Absolutely." His voice was husky.

"What scares you about them?"

"This…" He lowered his head and kissed her again.

This time the storm didn't interrupt them. Instead it energized them. As if the realization that they'd just cheated death made this moment all the more intense.

Their kiss was a heated exchange of sleek tongues and throaty murmurs as Striker explored every curve and corner of her mouth. Their embrace was a fiery seduction of caressing hands and appreciative touches as Striker explored every curve and corner of her body. He tugged her overshirt from the waistband of her skirt and slid it off her shoulders.

For a moment her arms were trapped. She had to remove her hold on his shirt in order to quickly slide her arms out. Now that she was free, she returned the favor, tugging on the pearlized snaps of his shirt. They flew open, allowing her to push the material off his shoulders.

The flashlight provided just enough light to prevent the darkness from closing in on her. And allowed her to see a hint of the muscled ridges of his bare chest. She brushed her fingers over the enticing warmth of his skin. His flesh quivered beneath her touch, making her feel incredibly powerful.

He felt so solid, so strong, yet he was reacting to her caresses as she was reacting to his. Without restraint.

His lean fingers slid beneath the hem of her sleeveless top, moving upward until he reached the clasp of her bra. Seconds later, she was freed of its silky confines. The roundness of her breasts filled his cupped palms. Her nipples tightened as he gently brushed his thumb over their tender peaks.

She murmured a protest when his lips left hers, but that was soon followed by a gasp of pleasure as seconds later those same lips hovered over her left breast. His warm breath bathed her skin, and left her waiting breathless for his next move. She didn't have long to wait. He swirled the wet tip of his tongue around the rosy tip before his lips closed around her, tugging her softly and oh-so-sweetly into his mouth.

The flow of warmth pulsed deep within her. She was drowning in a sea of reckless passion as he handled her with the utmost care, seducing her with the erotic suction. She clenched her fingers on his shoulders as blissful sensations rocked her world.

When his lips returned to hers, her tongue boldly tangled with his.

Striker moved even closer, urging her lower body into the cradle of his hips.

His hungry mouth, his hard body, his exploring hands all conveyed the nearly intolerable level of a man's desire.

Her parted lips, her throbbing body, her stroking fingers, all conveyed the rapidly escalating level of her own needs.

Seconds later, Striker was sitting on the pine bench again, with her on his lap. This time her legs were around his hips, her ruffled petticoat flowing over his hands as they gripped her upper thighs, the part of her that ached for him pressed against his throbbing arousal. He rocked her back and forward, creating an erotic friction against the taut placket of his jeans.

Kate distantly heard the sound of the cellar door opening, but it didn't really register. Until she heard the sound of Tony's voice.

"Are you two going to stay in that cellar all day?" Tony called out. "Come on up here. You've got company."

"Striker, are you down there?" a woman's voice asked. "It's your mother. Surprise!"

Chapter Seven

Kate leapt off his lap as if ejected from the cockpit of an F-16 fighter jet.

She refastened her bra in record time, and yanked her top back into place. Then her fingers lowered to hastily retuck her top into the waistband of her skirt.

Striker only knew all this because while he was blocking Kate from view with his body, he'd also taken several glances over his shoulder to see how she was doing.

"Hey, Mom, you sure know how to make an entrance," Striker called out, his voice rueful. "Give us a second here..." He reached out to help Kate tidy herself but she just batted his hands away and frantically pointed to his own undone shirt.

Thankfully Tony was distracting his parents with talk about damage done to the barn, and the horses all being unharmed. The rain that had poured down right after the twister had stopped.

Striker had refastened the snaps on his shirt although he left it untucked. He moved forward only to have Kate scramble past him and up out of the storm cellar with more speed than agility. He was immediately at Kate's side with a hand on her elbow, steadying her until they reached solid, albeit muddy, ground.

A moment later he was enveloped by his mom fiercely hugging him before quickly letting him go.

"Sorry about that," Angela said, stepping back and blinking away tears. "I didn't mean to get all emotional on you that way."

"That's okay." Striker glanced over at his dad, who looked like he'd rather chew glass than be standing here on the Westwind Ranch. Stan Kozlowski was solidly built, a Marine through and through who still proudly wore his hair in a buzz cut despite the fact that he was now retired.

"Nice weather you've got down here in Texas," his dad drawled. "Very impressive welcome." He nodded to the tree that lay splintered a short distance away.

"What? You don't know better than to be tooling around in an RV in a twister?" Striker countered. "It's not like you're driving a Humvee."

"No problem. The storm was ahead of us," his dad stated.

"I warned him that twisters have been known to turn around, but you know how your father is." Angela glanced at her husband with equal parts of affection and exasperation. "As to why we're here... I needed to come back and pay my respects." Her green eyes clouded with memories before she made a conscious effort to regain control. "I had no idea we'd arrive on the shirttails of a tornado."

"Never a dull moment, huh?" Striker gave his mom a quick hug.

Angela's smile reflected her appreciation. "We arrived to find Tony and some of the hands trying to haul this huge tree limb off the cellar doors.''

"Naturally I pitched in," his dad said.

Striker nodded. "Of course. A Marine never stands around waiting for others to get things done."

"I was wondering if you'd remember that, or if being a Texas oilman had changed your views." His father's voice reflected his disapproval.

"I am not a Texas oilman. I'm a Marine," Striker stated. "First and foremost."

"Then what the Sam Hill are you doing down here?" his dad demanded angrily.

"Avoiding a twister," Striker drawled.

"I didn't mean down there in the storm cellar, I meant down here in Texas and you know it."

"Can we hold off on this discussion until later, please?" his mom said. Focusing on Kate, she said, "Allow me to introduce myself. I'm Angela Kozlowski and this stubborn jarhead is my husband, Stan."

"I'm glad to meet you. I'm Kate Bradley."

"You're Jack's daughter?" Angela asked.

"That's right." Kate nodded. "He said you two practically grew up together."

"That's not all they practically did together," Stan growled. "He's an old beau of hers."

"You're exaggerating. Besides, that was a lifetime ago," Angela put a reassuring hand on her husband's muscular arm.

Striker's dad did not appear to be greatly appeased by her words.

"I really need to get over there and make sure my parents are okay," Kate said. She also wanted to escape this embarrassing situation of getting caught by Striker's parents making out with their son in the storm cellar.

"Call them on your cell phone," Striker said. "See if you can reach them that way."

"I have a feeling you won't be needing to do that," Tony said, tipping his head toward the long one-lane drive leading to the ranch. "That looks like them now."

Sure enough, their silver Lexus SUV was fast approaching the ranch house.

Kate's stomach tightened as she prayed that nothing was wrong, that her father hadn't sent over a ranch hand in the family SUV because her father's heart had given out. She held her breath until she saw him get out of the driver's seat. "We wanted to make sure everyone over here was okay after that twister," Jack said.

Kate hurried to his side, longing to hug her dad but knowing he wouldn't welcome such a public display. Instead she tried to stay calm. "I'm glad to see you both. Did the storm do any damage at our place?"

Jack shook his head. "No. It veered away, heading farther north." His eyes were on Angela. "I wasn't expecting to see you here."

"We just arrived," Angela replied. "How are you, Jack?"

"Can't complain," he said. "I'm sorry about your loss, Angela. I know you and your dad had your differences, but all the same, Hank loved you."

"The old man had a funny way of showing it," Stan growled.

"I can't deny that," Jack said.

"This is my husband." Angela made the introductions.

Jack nodded. "Nice to meet you."

The two men shook hands as if they were participants in a contest to see who was the most strong willed.

Kate wasn't sure who the winner was, but she did know that her mother was losing her temper. "Since my husband seems to have lost his manners, I apparently am left to introduce myself. I'm Elizabeth Bradley.''

Even in the aftermath of the terrible storm, with broken windows, cracked trees and downed branches all around them, Elizabeth still managed to maintain that elegant composure that was her trademark. The black linen slacks she wore contrasted strikingly with the red silk shirt she'd paired with it.

''Let's go inside,'' Angela suggested. ''Before it starts raining again.''

They all turned to look at the house, which had several broken windows but no other apparent structural problems.

''You were lucky the damage wasn't worse,'' Jack said.

When Angela slipped in the mud, Jack was the first one by her side, putting his hand on her arm to prevent her from falling.

''The damage is bad enough.'' Elizabeth's voice was icy.

''I agree.'' By contrast, Stan's voice was hot with disapproval.

''Jack, we really should get back home and leave these folks to get on with their family reunion,'' Elizabeth stated.

Stan didn't say anything, just joined Angela and placed a possessive arm around her shoulders.

''How long are you staying?'' Jack asked, his hand returning to his side.

''I'm not sure,'' Angela replied.

''Listen, why don't we all go out for dinner tomorrow evening?'' Jack suggested. ''I know a place down by the River Walk that serves the best margaritas in all of Texas. What do you say?''

''That sounds lovely,'' Angela said. ''Thank you.''

"Great." Jack smiled. "I'll make the reservations at Denada's. Seven sound okay?"

"Just ducky," Stan growled. "We'll meet you there."

"We could all go in my SUV." Jack nodded toward the Lexus.

"We'll go in our own vehicle."

Jack lifted a brow at the RV. "Parking space downtown is limited."

"Don't worry about us, we'll manage," Stan said.

"Yes, dear, don't worry about them." Elizabeth's displeasure was becoming more evident although her smile, the one that won her the title of Miss Texas, remained bright. "Come along, Jack." She put a possessive hand on his arm and tugged.

"We'll see you tomorrow then," Jack said. "Are you coming, Kate?"

She nodded, still surprised by the undertones between her parents and Striker's.

"Then you'd better come with us," Jack said. "It appears that silly little car of yours met its match."

For the first time, Kate glanced over to the area where her car was parked at the far side of the house. The roof of her spunky-yellow VW was crushed like a bug beneath the weight of the tree that had fallen on it.

"Oh, honey, I'm so sorry." Angela patted Kate's shoulder. "I'm so glad you weren't out driving in it when the storm hit."

Kate started to shake. She gripped her hands together and hid them in the folds of her skirt. She'd really loved that car. It had been something special, a spur-of-the-moment purchase that had been such fun. Something she'd done entirely on her own. Now it was crushed. "I'll call…" She had to pause and clear her throat to hide her trembling voice. "I'll call my insurance company and make arrangements to have it towed out of your way."

"I'll drive you back to the city," Striker said.

Jack frowned, clearly not a fan of that idea. "Electricity is out all over the city. The roads are blocked with downed trees. The authorities are asking that people stay off them unless it's an emergency. There's no need for you to drive Kate anywhere. She can come home with us."

"Of course she can," Elizabeth said. "Come along, Kate."

Kate felt as though she were between a rock and a hard place. In her current vulnerable state, she knew spending more time with Striker would be a dangerous thing. Yet she also feared that going with her parents had its hazards as well.

She was feeling emotionally exposed, her usual barriers swept away. Which meant her customary protective measures weren't in place to block her parents' unintentional but frequently hurtful comments.

The fact that it had been left to Angela, a relative stranger, to comfort her upon the discovery that her car had been crushed was no surprise. But it was a sad statement on the state of affairs between Kate and her parents. It would never have occurred to them to reach out to her.

Not that they didn't love her in their own way. They did. But their way was defined by expectations and responsibilities and not by hugs and reassurances.

In the end, Kate went with her parents, considering it the lesser of two evils.

Striker watched Kate go, wishing he knew what to say to make her feel better.

"She'll be okay," his mom said.

"I hope so." Striker watched her get into the luxury

SUV. Her white petticoat had mud on it now. He remembered seeing a glimpse of her legs earlier in the day, vividly recalled the ruffles flowing over his hands as he held her body intimately close to his.

"I'm going to stay out here and supervise the cleanup," Tony said, tilting his head toward the men who were already bringing sheets of plywood from the barn to board up the broken windows in the house.

"I'll help you," Striker and Stan said in unison.

"No, you both go with Señora Angela."

"It's good to see you again after all these years." Angela smiled at Tony. "I just wish it were under better circumstances."

Tony nodded before turning his attention to the men doing the cleanup.

It was only now hitting Striker that this was the house where his mom had grown up. It felt weird for him to be standing on the porch, trying to act like a host. Not knowing what to say, the best he could come up with was, "Consuela has the day off."

"Who's Consuela?" Stan asked.

"The housekeeper." Striker opened the front door and ushered them in.

"Of course." Stan nodded mockingly. "The housekeeper. What about the maid and butlers? They have the day off, too?"

Striker faced his dad. "You want to tell me what you're so bummed out about?"

"I don't approve of you being here."

"I'm just following—"

"—orders. Yeah, I know. Those orders stink. Your C.O. had no right making you come down here."

"Actually it wasn't my C.O.'s idea. It came from higher up the chain of command."

"I don't care if it came from the president himself. I

don't think these are lawful orders and I say we take your case to JAG headquarters.''

"Whoa." Striker held up his hands, surprised by his dad's outburst. "Hold on a second now."

"You're even starting to pick up a Texas accent. I fought Hank all those years, trying to keep hold of my sons and now that he's gone he still manages to…"

"To do what, Dad?" Striker challenged him to say what he really meant.

Stan did. Sort of. "I'd say you're enjoying yourself too much."

Striker's expression tightened. "Want do you want from me?"

"For you to do me proud."

His words stung. "I thought I'd already done that."

Growling under his breath, his dad pivoted on his heel and walked back out.

"Let him go," Angela said. "He didn't mean that. You know he's proud of you, Striker. Terribly proud."

"Then what's his problem?"

"I didn't realize how strongly Stan felt that Hank was competing with him, trying to take you away from us. I didn't realize how much he resented the fact that I had you and your brothers each come down here for one summer. He never said anything at the time, but then that's not his way. Instead he lets it build up over the years and then he blows up."

"So what are you going to do about it?"

"Nothing. He's not ready to listen to what I have to say yet. His anger would block out any explanation I make. I'll talk to him when he calms down."

Striker suddenly recalled Kate's comment earlier in the week about nothing going wrong…and his warning that saying nothing could go wrong was an invitation for trouble.

That had sure turned out to be the case. In the space of an hour he'd avoided being flattened by a tornado, made out with Kate, gotten caught by his mom, watched his parents fight over he still wasn't sure what and had his dad tell him that he was enjoying himself too much.

Yeah, right. Any more enjoyment like this and he'd be a dead man.

"You know, I never imagined my first time back in this house would turn out like this," his mom said.

Striker didn't know how to answer that so he stayed quiet.

"I haven't returned since I walked out to elope with your father." Her expression turned melancholy. "The last time I talked to my father was this past Christmas, when I called him to wish him happy holidays."

Her comment surprised him. "I didn't know you'd talked to him that recently. I hadn't had any contact with him at all since I joined the Marines. Every so often, I'd hear how he'd tried to lasso some general or other high-ranking official to complain about how the Marine Corps had brainwashed me into abandoning the oil business."

"My father hated to lose. You know how Marines hate to lose?"

Striker nodded.

"Well, multiply that by ten and you have how much my father hated to lose. I don't know." She shoved her short brown hair off her forehead. "Maybe I shouldn't have agreed to allow you to come down to the ranch before you joined the Marines. Maybe it would have been better to have cut off all contact entirely. But I just couldn't do that. I always thought that if the door was left open, maybe my father would walk through and meet me halfway. It's still hard to believe he's gone." She stared up at the large portrait of Hank that hung in the two-story-high foyer.

"Sometimes it feels as if he's watching over my shoulder," Striker admitted.

"Maybe he directed that twister our way as a little reminder for us to stay on our toes, hmm?" His mom's smile was a little unsteady.

"I wouldn't put it past him."

"He had his good moments," Angela said softly. "Just not enough of them. And after my mother died when I was nine, he became even more caught up with King Oil. It was as if his spending time there meant that he didn't have to deal with my mother's death at all. As long as he stayed busy with work, there was no time to think about personal loss."

Striker could understand that. "But what about later, after you'd married? He shouldn't have been so hard on you all those years."

"I'd disobeyed him. That was pretty much an unforgivable crime in his book."

"Yet you talked to him on the phone, called him to wish him happy holidays."

"Like I said, I'd hoped we could get over the past and move on. In the end there wasn't enough time to do that."

"Yeah, I know." He'd told himself that there would always be time to make things right with the old man, but it hadn't turned out that way. As usual, Hank had thrown a monkey wrench in the works.

"So how are you settling in at King Oil?" Angela asked him.

"I haven't blown anyone up yet."

His mom smiled. "That's a good thing."

"I suppose."

She tucked a hand in the crook of his arm. "Tell me about Kate."

"She was Hank's attorney and she's the executor of Hank's will."

"I know that much. I don't know why you were kissing her down in the storm cellar."

So his mother had seen more than he'd thought. "We'd just survived a tornado."

Angela appeared to be disappointed with his answer. "So kissing her was just a way of appreciating the fact that you were both still alive? Nothing more?"

"Why the inquisition?" Striker shifted restlessly. "You've never questioned me like this about my romantic history before."

"She seems like a nice young woman. I wouldn't want to see her get hurt. You do have a reputation with women, Striker. I may be your mother, but I know that you can be quite the charmer when you want to be."

"Gee, thanks."

"I also know that your duty as a Force Recon Marine comes first for you. And that there are dark places in your heart that you won't share with anyone and perhaps never will."

This conversation was making him very uncomfortable. "Hey, how about something to drink? Lemonade maybe? Consuela always has a pitcher of lemonade in the fridge."

He led his mom into the kitchen, where he belatedly remembered that the electricity was off. There was enough daylight left that it wasn't a problem yet, but it would be soon.

"I wonder if they still keep the candles...." His mom opened the pantry door and bent down to the lower shelf. "Yes, here they are." She pulled out several packs of candles of various sizes. "The storms here in Texas can be pretty vicious. It's always a good idea to be prepared."

Striker set her glass of lemonade on the large pine table and took a swig of the long-neck bottle of imported Mexican beer he'd gotten out of the huge Sub-Zero fridge for himself.

"This table is new," his mom murmured, running her hand over the rich wood before blinking away sudden tears. "And Tony, he has white hair. He was so young the last time I saw him. So many things have changed."

Striker hoped his mom wasn't going to cry. He could deal with enemy fire but he couldn't handle his mother in tears. Because she never cried. Not in front of him.

She'd had to handle numerous emergencies on her own, from his brother Ben's appendectomy at age ten to flooded basements and broken furnaces. All because his dad had been away on deployment—in South Korea or the Gulf or wherever else he was needed.

Angela had always managed. She'd always been strong. Until now. Now she looked like she wanted to cry. He watched her cautiously. "Hey, are you going to be okay?"

Her green eyes, so like his own and so like her father's, met his. "Absolutely." She blinked the sheen of tears away. "I'm sorry. I didn't mean to get all emotional on you this way." She took a calming sip of lemonade.

Now he felt bad, as if he'd stopped her from doing something she needed to. "If you really feel like, you know…like you have to…uh…to cry…uh…it's okay." He'd suck it up and manage somehow.

She smiled. "Thanks for giving me permission, but I'm okay now. I know you'd rather be out there with the men instead of sitting in here holding my hand, figuratively speaking."

The chirping sound of a cell phone came from Angela's purse, slung over the back of the pine chair. She answered and spoke briefly before handing the phone over to him. "It's your brother, Ben. He wants to talk to you."

"I just saw on the weather channel that several tornadoes have hit the San Antonio area. What are you doing down there, big brother? Sounds like you've really ticked off Mother Nature."

"Very funny. I thought you were heading out on a training mission?"

"We deploy first thing in the morning. Me and two thousand other Marines from Camp Lejeune. Should be a nice party."

"Try not to get into any trouble. I don't want you doing anything that would make me look bad." Striker couldn't help giving his younger brother a hard time. As the oldest, it was his duty to harass his siblings. They paid him back in kind.

"Hey, I'm not the one playing oil tycoon down there in Texas. You're the one who needs to stay out of trouble. Because I won't be there to save your butt when you get in a mess."

"Right," Striker scoffed. "Like that happens." But it was true that Ben was the caretaker in the family, the one who'd always brought home strays when he was kid, the one who always befriended those in need of a buddy.

"Take care of Mom while I'm gone. And listen, it's fine by me if you want to blow off this entire inheritance thing. I don't want Hank's money. Gotta go." A second later Ben had hung up.

"He told me to look after you," Striker told his mom.

"And I have no doubt that you'd do a good job of that. Not that I need looking after. After raising five boys and living in ten states in ten years, I can pretty well handle anything."

"How about seeing Tony in bunny slippers?" Striker teased her. "Are you sure you can handle that?"

Angela reached over to steal a swig of his beer. "Bring it on. After a day like today, bunny slippers are a mere drop in the bucket."

Kate didn't get much sleep that night. She could have chalked it up to surviving the tornado. But that was only part of it. A small part.

The major reason she was tossing and turning in her parents' guest room bed was because of what had happened down in the storm cellar. She'd blossomed from Ice Queen to Sultry Seductress and all because of Striker.

His touch did that to her—made her wild and reckless. Made her confident and confused.

Her body stirred at the memory of how and where he'd touched her. Her breasts were still sensitive, her nipples tightening at the vivid flashbacks playing in her mind of his tongue on her, his mouth surrounding hers.

She licked her lips at the image of her hands on his body, so smooth and powerful beneath her fingertips. How awesome it was to match that masculine strength with her feminine energy, marrying the two together.

During that time she'd stopped thinking, stopped worrying. Instead she'd simply lived, enjoyed, explored, satisfied and been satisfied.

Now that she'd experienced such joy, she wanted more. She wasn't willing to hide her emotions behind a wall any longer. She'd turned a corner, unsure where the road ahead led but knowing she didn't want to turn back.

That resolve remained with Kate the next morning as she sorted through a box of her old clothes in the closet. Her mom had told her the night before that she'd kept some of Kate's extra clothes still stored there. Kate unearthed a pair of jeans, and a San Antonio Spurs T-shirt from the year they'd won the NBA Championships. But she really hit pay dirt at the bottom, where she found a pair of boots.

They were the boots she'd worn that day she'd ridden out to the pond and first seen Striker all those years ago. They were brand-new then. No longer. The leather was nicked and worn. There was no shiny silver trim just for show. Instead the metal had the burnished patina caused by years of use. To her surprise, the boots still fit.

Kate entered the formal dining room more casually dressed than she had since she'd graduated from law school.

Her mother raised an eyebrow at her attire. "You really should keep some clothes here for situations like this."

"Situations like this?" Kate slid into a Windsor chair and added two pieces of toast to her Wedgwood china plate. "You mean when a tornado hits?"

"No, I mean when you have to stay over. In fact, I still don't understand why you insist on living in that tiny loft downtown."

Each time Kate came to her parents' home, she heard the same complaints. She tried to ignore the words, but doing so expended a lot of inner energy.

"The guest house here is bigger," her mother was saying.

Ah, but the condo is *mine,* Kate thought to herself. She needed some place to call her own, some *space* of her own.

"And you really should be thinking about your romantic future instead of wasting time on that Marine next door." Elizabeth was clearly on a roll this morning. "Babs Abbott called me and said that you haven't returned Rodney's phone calls. You know the Abbotts are one of the city's premier families and that Babs plays bridge with me. Your being rude to Rodney has created a very awkward situation for me.''

''Rodney and I have nothing in common.''

''How do you know that?'' Elizabeth demanded. ''You haven't even gone out with him.''

''We've run into each other several times at various gatherings.''

''Naturally. Rodney is an up-and-coming business-man.''

He was also a stuck-up, self-centered bore. Over the years since Ted's death, Kate had dated a number of men. But she'd always ended up alone. Because none of them was the *right* one. And this time she wasn't going to follow her parents' dreams and marry the man of their choice.

Throughout this time, her father remained silently ensconced behind his newspaper.

Kate needed to get away from the heavy burden of their expectations.

''I'm going for a ride on Midnight,'' she said abruptly. She grabbed some fruit from a bowl in the center of the table on her way out.

''I wasn't finished speaking with you, Katherine!'' Her mother's disapproving voice followed Kate.

She blocked it out.

It wasn't until the wind was rushing through her hair as she let Midnight have his way, galloping across the meadow away from the house and stables, that Kate realized how much she missed riding, missed the illusion of freedom.

The horse was older now, and so was she. No longer was she the seventeen-year-old with a secret crush on the sexy newcomer next door. The gelding was no

longer as high-spirited, but he welcomed the opportunity
to let loose. As did Kate.

As she rode, she noticed that the storm had indeed
missed this section of her parents' property. There were
no trees downed, no fallen branches to block their way.
Instead there was only open space in front of her and
Midnight.

How tempting it was to just keep riding and not go
back.

To leave the responsibilities, the emotional baggage
behind.

That wish had gotten her into trouble before. She'd
wanted to take off when Ted's car crashed.

But Kate was tired of dealing with her past. Just for
today she wanted to live in the moment. Was that too
much to ask?

Stop thinking, she ordered herself. Just *be*. Without
the stress of decision making.

She'd already taken care of the business of her
crushed car, calling her insurance agent and making arrangements. That was enough for today. Time for some
fun for a change.

The day was sunny and hot. The weather front that
had caused yesterday's violent storms was still perched
in the area, with more storms predicted but not until
later. A great day to wash her cares away in the pond
that bordered their property with Westwind.

Slowing her horse to a walk, Kate headed that way.
It wasn't until she'd dismounted and tied Midnight's
reins around a tree trunk that she realized she wasn't
alone.

Striker was already in the water, skinny-dipping as he
had been all those years ago. "Who's there?"

This time Kate didn't shirk away. She was no longer
an unsure teenager. She was a woman now.

"It's me." Confidently strolling forward, she grinned at him before quoting the woman who was very good at being bad—Mae West. "Is that a gun in your pocket, cowboy, or are you just happy to see me?"

Chapter Eight

"I'm not wearing any pockets." Striker's grin was downright wicked. "In fact, I'm not wearing anything at all."

"I had noticed that." Her own smile was a tad bit naughty.

"Did you now?"

"I did. But then attorneys are trained to observe little details like that."

"Hey, watch what you're calling a *little* detail. We Marines tend to be sensitive about the size of our...details."

"A sensitive Marine, huh? Next thing I know, you'll be wearing bunny slippers like Tony."

"Yeah, right. That'll happen when cows give beer."

Kate cracked up. "You've been getting lessons from Tex on good ol' Texas sayings again."

"Guilty as charged, ma'am."

Something had changed when he'd kissed her in the storm cellar yesterday and helped her deal with her claustrophobia. She'd turned a corner somehow. She was tired of being afraid. She wanted to just live, not worry about what could go wrong and instead, enjoy what was going right.

So here she was, flirting with a naked man. And not just any man, but Striker.

He stood, the water level just below his waist. "I'm aimin' on comin' out now." His Texas drawl was good. The gleam in his green eyes was very, very bad.

"Go right ahead." She met his challenge with one of her own.

"Want to hand me that towel hanging on the branches over there by my clothes?"

She did as he asked, noting that he was a white briefs guy. Then she made the mistake of pausing to take a peek over her shoulder to see what he was up to. Wow. She blushed but didn't look away, fascinated by the interplay of rippling muscles as he strolled forward with the self-assured step that was unequivocally his. Even when naked as a jaybird.

He took the towel from her and placed it around his hips.

Kate sank onto a nearby log, grateful for its presence since her knees had suddenly given out.

Wow.

She closed her eyes, reliving the moment, but in doing so missed watching him get dressed, which was a good thing. She was still new to this seductress stuff and didn't want to overdo things her first time out. Even so, there was something seductive about hearing him dress, the slide of his legs into his jeans, the sound of him zipping them up.

"You can look now." There was more than a hint of laughter in his voice.

Her eyes flew open. He'd put on a brightly colored

Hawaiian shirt but hadn't bothered to button it up. He looked yummy enough to eat.

No, *yummy* was too cute somehow. Striker wasn't cute. He was so much more than that. There wasn't a pretty-boy bone in his awesome body.

Okay, she had to think about something else or she'd start drooling here. She needed a moment to regain her composure. Time for a change of subject.

Something neutral. His parents. The ranch. Yes, those were good topics. *Go ahead, Counselor.* "How are things at Westwind today? Are things getting back to normal?"

"If you call my dad sleeping out in the RV instead of coming into the house *normal,* then yeah, things are back to normal at Westwind."

"Was it too hard on your mom being back after all this time?"

He sat beside her on the log before replying. "My mom stayed in the house. It was only my dad who refused to step foot in Hank's house. My mom claims she slept like a baby."

"Do you believe her?"

He shrugged. "I don't know. Both my parents are acting strange. How about yours?"

"My mother disapproves of acting strange. It's not something that a former Miss Texas does."

"I didn't realize your mom was a former beauty queen."

"Do me a favor and don't use that terminology at dinner tonight. She doesn't like the term *beauty queen.*"

He raised an eyebrow. "Why not? She struck me as the regal type. Is that where you get it from?"

"Me?" Kate shook her head. "I'm nothing like my mother. She looks perfect in any situation."

"And you don't? The first time I met you I wanted

to take your hair down out of that fancy perfect twist you had it pinned up in.''

"You were glaring at me as if you wanted to throttle me.''

He smiled wolfishly. "I definitely wanted to get my hands on you.''

She wasn't about to act like a prim miss. She didn't blush or look away. Instead she asked, "Why?''

"Why what?''

"Why did you want to get your hands on me?''

"I don't know.'' He leaned forward to nuzzle her throat with the tip of his tongue. "Why do you want my hands on you?''

"Because it feels good.''

"Yeah, that would be my answer, too.''

The kiss began in the middle of her forehead and gradually took in her eyes, the curve of her cheeks, the tip of her nose before hovering over her mouth. He gently caught her bottom lip between his teeth, drawing it into his mouth to suck and nibble, priming her for the deeper thrusts of his tongue that were yet to come.

His hands were equally seductive and creative, tunneling beneath the golden mass of her hair to gather the strands in one fist while his other hand slipped beneath her T-shirt to trail up her spine. He was in no hurry. His leisurely pace educated her senses about the infinite pleasures to be had by going slowly.

She had no idea. He explored every inch of her bare back, pausing to fingerpaint invisible paintings on her skin, a swirl here, a line there. Every place he touched hummed with excitement.

And all the while his mouth continued its passionate play—tempting, exploring, sharing.

Striker felt as if he'd stumbled into the pot of gold at the end of a rainbow. He'd come out here to the pond to be alone. To think. To remember how good Kate felt in his arms.

And then she'd shown up. In her sexy jeans and Spurs T-shirt. Ready and more than willing to meet him half-way.

It was as if the tornado yesterday had swept away the old Kate and replaced her with the new one, the one who gave as good as she got.

There was no resisting her now.

She slid his shirt off his shoulders and ran her fingers over his bare skin. He groaned. Who knew it would be this good? Who knew it *could* be this good?

He released her hair to tug his shirt off and pull her closer. The thin cotton of her T-shirt provided little pro-tection. He felt the familiar brush of her taut nipples against his flesh and longed to touch them again.

But before he could do so he was interrupted by the feel of something cold and wet pressed against his back, almost knocking him right off the log.

"What the…!" Striker leapt to his feet only to turn and find a huge black horse glaring at him

"Midnight must have gotten lonely," Kate said. "I tied him up but he must have gotten loose. He has a thing for apples. Don't you, big boy."

It took Striker a second to realize that she was calling the horse *big boy,* not him. Then he registered the rest of her comment.

"You brought food?"

Kate nodded, patting the backpack she'd dropped on the ground when she'd first arrived.

"I'm starving," Striker said. "I left without eating breakfast."

"Me, too," she confessed.

"Yeah, well, with our parents both acting weird we may have our hands full at this dinner tonight. My dad

told my mom to cancel. She told him to grow up. Those
were the last words they spoke. I left after an hour of
being intermediary. My dad wasn't real pleased with me
anyway.''

"He wasn't?" She handed Striker an apple.

She looked like Eve sitting there with her lips swollen
from his kisses, her face flushed by passion, her golden
hair rumpled by his hands. A smart footloose man would
recognize trouble when he saw it and walk away. Before
things got out of hand. Before he got in over his head.

But Striker had never been one to back away from
trouble. He took the apple.

"Why is your dad upset with you?" Kate asked.

"He doesn't approve of this entire situation. Me being
at King Oil. The inheritance. He doesn't want any of us
to accept any money from Hank's estate.''

"And what do you want?"

"To kiss you again.''

Striker tasted like apple. He'd barely begun kissing
her when Midnight butted his head against Striker's bare
back once again. "Your horse is jealous.''

"You know what I need?"

"To get rid of your horse.''

"No.''

"Just get him out of the way for a while.''

"No.''

"For me to kiss you right here?" He pressed his lips
against the hollow in her throat.

"No.'' She suddenly sat up almost dislodging him. "I
need to go home. To my condo. And I need you to take
me there.''

His smile was downright wolfish, his green eyes
gleaming with anticipation. "You're inviting me to your
place? To continue this?"

"No. I'm sorry, I didn't mean to give you the wrong

CATHIE LINZ · 123

CATHIE LINZ · 123

impression. I meant that if we're all going out to dinner tonight then I do need to get organized and get ready.''

"And get away from your parents. Hey, I can understand that. Do you need a lift?''

"I rode my horse here, remember?''

"I meant from your parents' to your place in the city. Since your car is out of commission.''

She nodded. "I'd appreciate a lift, thanks.''

"Great. Then be prepared to embark at 1600 hours.''

"What?''

"Be ready to leave by four. I'll pick you up at your parents' place in the truck. Or I could drive the RV if you really want to drive your folks nuts.''

"I don't want to drive them nuts, I just want them to accept me the way I am.''

Despite the fact that Striker didn't pick her up in the RV, her mother was still disapproving as she looked out the window to where Striker was just pulling up. "I think you're spending entirely too much time with that Marine.''

"He's Hank's grandson,'' Jack pointed out.

"He's a Marine.''

"A very rich one.''

"I don't understand why we have to have dinner with these people,'' Elizabeth said.

"And I don't understand why you're getting so upset about this,'' Jack countered, giving his wife a disapproving look.

"I don't want to go.''

"Fine. Then stay home. I'll go without you.''

His words clearly surprised Elizabeth.

"Go ahead,'' Jack told Kate. "Don't keep Striker waiting for you. I'll see you at the restaurant tonight.

Call me when you get back to your condo,'' he added. "Just so I know you got home okay.''

Kate was touched that her father was concerned about her safety. Until he added, "We can discuss that Harper Enterprises file you took home with you.''

"It's always about work with you, isn't it?'' Elizabeth said. "Aren't you the least bit concerned for your daughter's well-being?''

"Of course I am. That's why I told her to call me. Besides, I know she's safe with Striker.''

"How do you know that?'' Elizabeth demanded.

"Because he's a Marine. He's trained to handle all kinds of situations.''

Kate had rarely seen her parents argue. They'd always been in perfect accord about their goals and expectations. She was totally unprepared as to how to handle this situation. Except to make her escape.

"You lit out of there as if your hair was on fire, to quote Tex,'' Striker noted as he held the passenger door open for her. "What's going on?''

"My parents are still arguing. They never argue.''

"Same here. Well, that's not exactly true. My parents are human, they argue about things sometimes. But I've never seen them acting so weird.''

For the first time she noticed that Striker was already dressed for dinner. He was wearing black pants, a white shirt, and a black leather bola tie. Glancing down at his attire, he grinned. "I was tempted to wear one of my Hawaiian shirts tonight just to see if anyone was paying attention.''

"I'm paying attention,'' Kate said. "You look very nice.''

"I figured it was stupid to drive all the way back here to change and then drive back into the city again. I thought I'd wait while you do whatever you need to do to get ready and then I'll come take you to the restaurant. I don't have to wait at your place if you don't want me to. I can take a walk or something. No big deal.''

It was a big deal. She didn't often have men come over to her place. It was her sanctuary. She usually met them on neutral ground.

And since her father's heart attack, she'd really been consumed with work, doing everything she could to get her dad back on his feet again. There hadn't been much time to devote to a personal life.

Not that she'd planned it that way. Somehow the time had just slipped by, going by so quickly that it was a little disconcerting.

Objection, Your Honor. The witness is thinking too much.

''You're welcome to wait at my place while I change,'' Kate said.

''I'd give you that old line about not changing too much, that I like you the way you are, but I realize you deserve better than that. Unfortunately, I can't think of anything suitably impressive at the moment.''

''You? At a loss for words? That has to be a first.''

''You've left me speechless several times, Kate.''

''Is that a bad or a good thing?''

''I'm not sure. I guess we'll find out sooner or later.''

''I guess we will.''

It reassured her somehow that Striker was no more certain of what was happening between them than she was. But he seemed willing to pursue it.

During the drive, they talked about King Oil and the changes he'd already set in place. Kate heard the excitement in his voice and was thrilled by it.

Just as she'd hoped, Striker was enjoying the work, whether he admitted it or not. And he was good at it.

He had the ability to inspire confidence in others. That was only one of his leadership abilities.

Their conversation made the trip into the city go by quickly. Kate's condo was located downtown, not too far from the River Walk. Instead of going for one of the high-rise condos, she'd selected a loft in an older, recently renovated building. The carved stone over the doorway and wrought iron around the windows were indications of a time when European craftspeople immigrated to San Antonio.

Kate loved the intricate woodwork in her loft as well as the light flowing in from the big windows. The pine floor had a wonderful glow to it when the sun hit it. She didn't have a lot of furniture yet—a big comfy couch with rounded arms, two chairs that she'd found at an antique store and had slipcovered and a handmade pine coffee table. Her TV and stereo were hidden behind an intricately carved cupboard. Her CDs were stored in what had once been a card-catalog cabinet in a library.

"Nice place," Striker said.

"Thanks." She'd taken great pleasure in decorating it herself. She'd wanted something that reflected her tastes—a place where she could feel comfortable, where everything was meant to be touched, used and enjoyed. The paintings on the walls all had personal meaning for her, from the large watercolor of mountains done by a professional artist friend of hers to the small oil painting of Texas wildflowers that she'd picked up at the Starving Artists Show along the River Walk last year.

Maybe that's why she was so particular about whom she invited into her private domain. Because it revealed things about her, about her likes, about the importance of creature comforts without ostentatiousness.

"Would you like something to drink?"

He shook his head. "I'm fine."

"Well, then. I guess I'll go get ready."

Kate climbed the stairs leading to the upper level where the master suite was located. The focal point of her bedroom was the carved and painted Victorian bed that she'd spotted in a shop window. She'd piled beautiful ecru and rose pillows on the floral comforter, creating a romantic oasis. An ivory ceramic chandelier hung from the high ceiling. The bedroom was protected from view by a series of hand-painted screens that picked up the ivory-and-rose color scheme.

She used the phone on her bedside table to call her dad and assure him she was home, before adding that she didn't have time to talk about the Harper file. She hung up before her father could protest too much.

As she disrobed in preparation for hopping into the shower, the realization that she was standing naked upstairs while Striker was right downstairs was more than a little disconcerting. Afterward, she quickly dressed in the still-steamy bathroom.

Kate had grabbed the first suitable outfit from her closet, a matching skirt and top in a body-hugging stretch jersey material. The burgundy color was a favorite of hers. The flattering gathers at the V-neck collar showed off her liquid silver-and-turquoise necklace. She added a wide, black leather belt with a silver buckle to complete the look.

Since they were walking the several blocks to the restaurant, she chose a comfortable pair of black leather boots instead of the strappy black high heels she often paired with this outfit. The slit in the skirt revealed a generous amount of her tanned leg each time she took a step.

She lifted her hair away from her face with two silver hair clips that matched the scrolled design on her belt. Her eye shadow and lipstick were in earthen shades and gave her a more seductive look somehow. Or maybe that was due to the fact that she was thinking about Striker.

He'd made himself comfortable on her denim couch and was paging through a coffee table book she had on the Alamo.

His gaze lifted the moment she entered the room and he immediately rose to his feet. His eyes didn't sweep over her body, they roamed from her head to the tips of her boots and back up again. He was eyeing her with unmistakable appreciation and passion. "You look great."

"Thanks."

He took a few steps closer, so that he could reach out with his index finger to gently touch the necklace nestled at the base of her throat. Slivers of excitement shot through her body. "You wore this to the barbecue yesterday. Did someone special give it to you?"

She nodded.

He expression turned brooding as his hand dropped to his side.

"It was a gift from me to me," she said.

His slow smile warmed her heart. "I'm glad to hear that."

Then, because Kate was unaccustomed to being the subject of such intensely sensual attention, she glanced down at the book he'd been studying. "Have you been to the Alamo yet?"

Striker shook his head. "I haven't had the time. There's this slave driver of a lady lawyer who never gives me a moment's peace."

"Well, she's offering to show you the Alamo tonight. It's on our way and we've got time if we leave now. Come on." She slipped her hand in the crook of his arm and tugged him toward the door.

Striker found he liked being led by a laughing Kate

as she proudly began reciting information about the cradle of Texas liberty. All he knew about it had been learned from the John Wayne movie he'd caught on a classic-movie cable station once.

"It was actually the first of several missions that Spanish friars established along the river in the early 1700s." He listened as she told him about the battle between Mexicans and Texas settlers in 1836. Santa Anna's troops had greatly outnumbered the Americans. Over 180 died, including Davy Crockett and James Bowie. "There's some speculation that the men could possibly have escaped, slipped away in the night. But they didn't. Instead they stayed and fought to the death."

Striker could understand that. Sometimes the price of freedom was high.

As he stood before the golden limestone face, he recognized that this was a place that stood for something. The nicked, weathered walls retained the spirit of the battle that had taken place there—the lives lost, the future changed. He could almost hear the echo of cannons from the distant past.

Kate didn't speak as she walked through the mission chapel with him. There wasn't any need for words. They simply shared the experience.

They passed the gift shop on their way out. "The Alamo doesn't get any federal funds. The Daughters of the Republic of Texas, whose members trace their lineage back to the original citizens of the republic, manage it," she said. "No fees are charged to visitors."

"Where do they get the money to maintain it?"

"From sales at the gift shop, donations and fundraising events."

Before leaving, Striker put a sizable amount in one of the donation boxes. From one warrior to so many others who'd died.

They crossed the Alamo Plaza and headed for the River Walk. Striker held her hand, as he had since they'd left her loft.

Kate was both humbled and exhilarated by the joy to be had from the simple contact. From time to time he'd run his thumb over the back of her fingers as if wanting to tell her how much he enjoyed touching her.

"This is nice," he murmured.

She thought he was referring to the River Walk, which was indeed the pride and joy of the city. "If you think it's nice now, you should see it during the holiday season, when they decorate all these trees with lights."

"I meant us. This." He lifted their entwined hands.

Nice was much too pedestrian a word for it. *Incredible* came a little closer. Not knowing what to say, she stayed silent.

"What?" he teased her. "No quick comeback from the lady lawyer?"

"The lady lawyer has the night off."

"I'm glad to hear it."

They shared a smile in the midst of the crowd. Couples and families mingled as they moved along the cobblestone walkways that ran beside the waterway or walked over the quaint bridges that crossed over it. Some stopped to read the menu of one of the many sidewalk cafés, while others paused to view the goods offered by the variety of specialty shops. Barges filled with tourists floated by. No one was in a hurry.

The predicted storms hadn't developed, but instead a cooling breeze rustled the leaves in the trees. The weather front was moving through without any further mayhem other than a chilling shift in the wind.

Kate tugged the shawl a little tighter around her shoulders.

Striker noticed her actions. "Are you cold?" Without

waiting for an answer, he placed his arm around her and gently tugged her closer. "There. Is that better?"

Kate nodded. It was heaven. Or as close to it as she'd ever been.

Every time she was with Striker, it got better. There were so many layers she was discovering, from that explosive first kiss in the King Oil headquarters to the heated embrace in the storm cellar to the flirtatious fun by the pond. And now this new dimension. The simple but deeply satisfying pleasure of his arm around her as they walked along the River Walk.

Both their parents were already seated at the restaurant by the time Kate and Striker arrived.

Kate could tell that her mother had taken extra care with her appearance. Elizabeth only wore her sapphire heart necklace, the one that Jack had given her for their thirtieth anniversary, when she wanted to make an impression. The black dress was an elegant Donna Karan design. Her blond hair fell in a smooth curtain around her face.

Striker's mother looked equally lovely in a different way. Not as artificial, more natural. Her short brown hair was a little windblown. She wore no jewelry other than a watch and her gold wedding ring. There was no designer label on her denim dress but it fit her well. Her green eyes were vibrant against her lightly tanned face.

The two men were equally different, with Jack's expensive Ralph Lauren look versus Stan's simple black pants and white shirt.

Striker held Kate's chair out for her, seating her before sitting down himself. Chips and salsa were already at the table. After checking with her, Striker ordered a margarita for Kate and a beer for himself.

The male jockeying for dominant alpha position between Jack and Stan began right off the bat with ordering the meal.

"I recommend the chicken enchiladas verdes, Angela," Jack said.

"Angela doesn't like chicken," Stan said. "We'll have the steak fajitas."

"The plates here are the size of Roman battle shields and they fill them up, so you may not be able to finish it all," Jack warned.

"I have a big appetite," Stan replied. "I'm sure I can handle whatever they give me."

"Really, Jack." Elizabeth's voice reflected her displeasure. "I think they can figure out what to order on their own."

"Ignore them," Striker leaned close to whisper in Kate's ear. "Tell me what you like."

"Wh-what?" He was using that seductive tone, the one that made her insides melt.

"What you like. From the menu." He pointed to the tri-fold paper she held in front of her.

So he was trying to distract her, was he? Well, two could play at that game. "I could make some suggestions, but I'd need to know how hot you like it."

He grinned. My, how that changed his face, making him even more sexy. His vivid green eyes sent her secret messages. Did he look at every woman this way? Well, not *every* woman maybe, but the ones he was interested in flirting with. Or was this special?

Striker wasn't a smooth ladies' man, but he had a powerful way about him and a boatload of charm. He also had another side he kept hidden, disguising his inner thoughts and his true emotions well.

No doubt that was due to his work as a Force Recon Marine. She'd already ascertained that trust was something that didn't come easily for him. The same was true for her.

Yet here they both were, flirting behind the cover of a menu while their parents bickered on the other side of the table.

"How hot do I like it?" Striker repeated her question. "The hotter the better. How about you?"

"I prefer all things in moderation."

"The problem with being moderate and careful is that you could miss something really good along the way."

Their conversation was interrupted by the arrival of their server who took their orders. In the end, Striker had the fajitas while Kate selected a chicken dish with mole sauce.

The food was excellent. The portions were huge. The conversation was competitive and dominated by Jack and Stan as they played a game of verbal one-upmanship that left Kate shaking her head in disbelief.

Kate had never seen her father behave this way before. Sure, he liked weaving a story. And, being a Texan, he liked elaborating on the truth a little. But he'd never gone at it quite this intensely.

"Then there was the time I was on safari in Kenya and saved our group from a charging rhino at considerable risk to myself."

Stan waited until Jack had finished his lengthy story before saying, "That's nothing. Talk to me after you've been involved with a ship takedown in the Persian Gulf."

"When you've traveled the world the way I have—"

"And what way would that be?" Stan interrupted him. "Being pampered at a bunch of fancy hotels?"

"As opposed to the high-class places you've been?" Jack countered with a raised brow.

"That's it! I've had it!" Elizabeth stated, rising to her

feet and tossing her napkin onto the table in disgust. "You two good ol' boys go right ahead and continue playing this verbal 'mine is bigger than yours' game. I've had enough. I'm leaving."

"An excellent idea," Angela said, getting to her feet as well. "I've had enough as well."

A second later both women had walked out of the restaurant and disappeared in the passing crowd along the River Walk.

Kate was speechless.

Striker wasn't. "We're taking off as well." He placed a handful of large bills on the table. "That should cover my meal and Kate's. My parents' as well."

"Put your money away. The meal is on me," Jack insisted.

Striker shook his head. "I pay my own way. And my family's."

Striker hustled Kate out of the restaurant so fast she didn't even get a chance to say goodbye. Looking over her shoulder, she saw her father and Stan look at each other with a shared expression of male confusion.

"We can't just leave them alone like that," she protested even as Striker ushered her through the door and out onto the River Walk.

"Sure we can. We just did."

"Are you sure they'll be okay?" Kate craned her head to try and catch sight of her dad through the large window.

Striker tugged her away. "They'll be fine."

"What if they start arguing again?"

"They're grown-ups. They'll manage."

"Your dad won't punch my dad or anything, will he?"

"I sure hope not."

"That's not very reassuring. I think we should go back."

"And I think you should stop worrying about your father and start concentrating on your own life."

"What do you mean?"

"I mean that your dad is a big boy and can take care of himself. You don't have to worry about him."

"He had a heart attack two years ago and almost died."

"I know. You told me. You also told me that he's doing fine now and that his latest checkup went great, right?"

"Yes, but…"

"No *buts*. That skunk just ain't gonna mate."

Kate cracked up.

"What are you laughing at? You don't think that sounds like a good Texas saying? One that Tex would approve of?"

"I don't think you live your life waiting for someone else's approval."

"You've got that right."

"Yet you automatically had that approval because you followed in your dad's footsteps and went into the Marines. What if you had wanted to be… I don't know…an artist or something?"

"You've clearly never seen me try and draw anything," Striker noted dryly. "I can manage a map but that's about it."

"You know what I mean."

"I like to think my parents would have supported my decision."

"Yet you told me that your dad is very upset about you working at King Oil."

"You didn't let me finish. And even if they didn't, I'd do whatever I needed to do anyway. There comes a point where you have to be true to yourself. You have to live the life you want to instead of the one expected of you.''

Easier said than done, Kate thought to herself.

She tried to shove those thoughts out of her mind as she and Striker stopped at several shops along the River Walk before giving in to temptation and getting some ice cream. But even while sitting beside him on a bench along the river, his words continued to repeat themselves in her mind.

Striker noticed her silence and commented on it when they entered her building a while later. ''You've been awfully quiet.''

''I've been thinking.''

''You do too much of that. You need to do more of this…'' He lowered his head and brushed his lips across hers.

The kiss blossomed into a sensual exploration of various angles and delicious moves. The world faded away as pleasure filled every particle of her body.

''Ahem. Sorry to interrupt…'' Angela said.

Kate's eyes flew open…to find not only Striker's mom, but her own mother standing a mere five feet away.

Chapter Nine

Kate knew what her mother was going to say. She could hear her already... *Really, Kate, you shouldn't be standing out here in the hallway where anyone walking by might see you making out with that Marine.*

Instead her mom surprised her by saying, "Angela and I had the best time tonight. I showed her some of my favorite shops in Rivercenter. They were doing a makeover clinic at the Lancôme counter so we stopped there and afterward we talked over a cup of latte."

"I've missed girl talk," Angela confessed. "Raising five sons means you don't get much feminine input."

"Darn right," Striker muttered, staring at his mom as if she'd turned into an alien from another planet.

"I had so much fun this evening. Thank you, Elizabeth." Angela hugged her. "It was so sweet of you."

"Nonsense." Elizabeth hugged her back. "I'm glad we were able to spend time together."

"Remember what I told you. Jack's tales about my being his first love were all a bunch of cow manure. The only time we kissed, we were both fourteen, and it was like kissing my brother…if I had one."

"Yuck!" Striker looked as his mother with the horrified expression of a son. "Too much information."

Angela laughed. "Have you noticed, Elizabeth, how children have this silly notion that they somehow were hatched out of a cabbage patch and that their parents never…"

"It's getting late," Striker interrupted. "I'd better drive you back to Westwind." He hustled his mom away.

Elizabeth watched him and stunned Kate even more by noting, "That is one fine-looking man."

"How many margaritas did you have tonight?" Kate asked suspiciously.

Elizabeth shrugged prettily. "I'm not sure."

"I'd better drive you home."

"No. I don't want to go home tonight. Would it be okay if I stayed in your guest room?"

"Sure." Kate unlocked her door and ushered her mom inside. "But we have to call Dad and tell him that you're here so he won't worry."

"It would serve him right if he did worry. Putting me through such misery, making me think he regretted marrying me and wishing he'd hooked up with Angela instead."

"What made you think a ridiculous thing like that?"

"Gee, honey, tell me what you really think." Her mom's voice was mocking.

"I'm sorry. I didn't mean to insinuate that your feelings were ridiculous. I just meant that Dad loves you. He always has."

Elizabeth sat on the denim couch and swapped the pillows, moving the floral one to the front. "He takes me for granted."

"Have you talked to him about any of this?" Kate placed her keys in the wooden bowl she kept on the foyer table for that purpose. As distracted as she was, she had to keep to her routine. She glanced at the hammered silver Mexican mirror on the wall over the table and discovered that her hair clips were totally lopsided thanks to Striker's caressing hands.

Her entire world was feeling lopsided at the moment. Her mother never came to visit her. She'd seen the loft once when Kate had first moved in, and that was it. Since she'd tried to strong-arm Kate into using her decorator, Kate hadn't been real eager to have her return.

But tonight was different. Her mom was different. Even if she was still rearranging Kate's throw pillows to her own liking.

"Talk to your father? Impossible. You know how he is. He hides behind that newspaper of his in the morning, then heads out to work, and when he gets home his mind is still on his caseload or his golf game. I'm just an accessory, like the dining room drapes or the Oriental carpet in the living room."

"I think you should talk to him."

"Tomorrow. I've had enough stress for one day." Elizabeth stood, looking at Kate uncertainly. "If you don't mind, I think I'll head off to bed."

"I don't mind. I'll call Dad for you."

"You do that." Elizabeth patted her cheek. "I may not tell you often enough, but I do love you, you know."

Emotion clogged Kate's throat and she had to blink away tears.

"You do know that, right?" Elizabeth said.

"It's nice to hear it," Kate confessed unsteadily.

"I know I'm not a real touchy-feely kind of person. That's not the way I was raised. It's not the way your father was raised. It's not the way we raised you. I'm thinking now that maybe that was wrong of us. We should have hugged you more.''

''I never doubted that you and Dad love me.'' What Kate doubted was that they were proud of her, that they would be happy for her to live the life she chose rather than the one they chose for her.

''Good. I'm glad to hear that.'' Elizabeth patted Kate's cheek one final time before yawning daintily. ''Good night, then.''

Striker didn't know what to say to his mom during the drive back to Westwind so he kept quiet. His mother talked enough for both of them.

She started off railing about the denseness of some men, then their competitiveness, then the forgotten fun to be had at a makeup counter.

This only convinced Striker even more that the woman in his truck was not really his mother. Aliens must have replaced her with a clone. Sure, under the fancy makeup, she still looked like his mom. But she sure wasn't *acting* like her.

Maybe this was due to the fact that she was back in Texas. Maybe it had put some kind of weird spell on her. A makeup spell. Next she'd get big hair.

''I know what you're thinking,'' she was saying.

''I doubt that.''

''You're thinking that I'm not acting like myself, right?''

''Right.''

''That's not a bad thing.''

''If you say so.''

''I do.'' She peered at him through the semidarkness. ''I can't tell what you're thinking anymore. I don't often know what you're thinking. Of all my sons, I do believe you are the most enigmatic. Not as enigmatic as your father, thank heavens.''

"I'm working on it.''

He'd meant it as a teasing comment, but she took it seriously. "Don't do that. Don't work on it. Hiding your feelings is not always a good thing. Not where the woman in your life is concerned. I like Kate, by the way. I guess I told you that already. But the more time I spend with her, the more I like her.''

"You spent more time with her mother than you did with Kate tonight.''

"True.''

"Are you sure you're not acting this way because of the stress of being back here in Texas? At being back at the ranch after so long?''

"What do you mean 'acting this way'? What way would that be? Standing up for myself?''

"No, you always do that.''

"I should hope so. Otherwise I'd be overrun by a houseful of Marines.''

"Understood. A Marine's wife needs to be strong. Strong enough to buck your father's orders.''

"I don't regret doing that, you know. I never have. I have regretted that my father couldn't get past that. Couldn't meet me halfway. And I deeply regret that we ran out of time.''

"He probably would have been thrilled to see you walking out of that restaurant tonight.''

"He probably would have sided with the men. He was a terrible chauvinist.''

"Yet he hired Kate as his attorney.''

"He must have mellowed some in his old age. Maybe your father will mellow, too. It could happen.''

"Yeah, when cows—''

"—give beer,'' they said in unison before laughing.

Apparently, Tex wasn't the only one with a colorful phrase or two up her sleeve.

The next week flew by as Striker really got down to business with King Oil. He created a combat team to battle corporate waste so that no employees would have to be laid off. He established a weekly strategy session with top executives. He cut response times in half—no more waffling over decisions, hiring expensive consultants to write thick reports, waiting years for something to happen. Forget that.

He'd just said as much to the top executives at this week's meeting.

"The Marine Corps leaves everyone else in the dust when it comes to turnaround time and pace," Striker told them. "The organization that moves faster, without sacrificing competence, has the edge over the competition."

He put a freeze on top management's expense accounts, putting an end to their lavish spending. And prepared new contracts stating that no longer would bonuses be distributed regardless of the company's well-being.

Striker took a day to meet with the lower-level managers who ran the day-to-day operations, following a meeting with the bean-counters in the accounting department. He spent the next day with the men out in the field; he met with engineers who wanted to purchase new equipment and talked to geologists.

But one of the most important things he did was assemble a talented group of people around him. The same way that any individual Marine was only as good as the team around him, Striker knew that the company needed to promote new ways of thinking instead of the stagnant rules of the past.

Luckily the people were already there. They often

weren't in charge, but they were ready to pitch ideas, to work on financial reports without resorting to creative but illegal means of juggling numbers.

Charles was not a happy camper about any of these developments. He especially disliked Striker's most recent order that each department head learn about the people in their section who made things work.

"What do you mean, learn about them?" Charles demanded. "Like who their family is? Where they were born?"

"I mean what they do for the company. Get as close to the frontline workers as possible."

Charles looked down his aristocratic nose. "We're not at war here. There is no front line."

"The battle is to keep King Oil going. You need to listen with an open mind and learn what works, what changes need to be made to make this one of the best private companies in the country. Why did the people in your department come work for us instead of going somewhere else?"

"Why do we care?" Charles countered. "They wanted a paycheck. What's the big deal?"

"The big deal is that you're only as good as your weakest link. An I-don't-get-paid-to-think mentality does not help any of us. A Marine recruit's problem-solving skills are an important part of the final stage of their training. Everyone needs to be capable of making decisions that lead the unit to accomplish its mission. It requires creative ability to devise a practical solution."

"We don't have time to do all these projects you're starting."

"Everyone else seems to have time, Charles. You're the only one who seems to have a problem."

"I'm warning you that if you keep up this ridiculous

imitation of the Marine Corps you're going to lose people.''

"Anyone in particular?"

"Me."

There. Charles had finally tossed the gauntlet on the table after weeks of veiled innuendoes.

The smirk the V.P. had on his face was a clear indication that he expected Striker to back down. Big mistake.

"I agree with you, Charles. And I've been meaning to talk to you about that."

"I'm glad to hear that." He leaned back in his chair, puffing out his chest with pride.

"I agree that since you obviously aren't happy any longer here at King Oil that it would be best for you to leave."

"Leave?"

"That's right. To resign."

"Are you crazy? This place wouldn't last five minutes without me."

"As a matter of fact, it lasted decades before you got here, and I have a feeling it's going to do just fine without you."

Charles's face turned red with anger. "I don't believe this!"

"Believe it."

"Fine. Go ahead and try to manage King Oil. You'll run this company into the ground. It's better I leave this sinking ship now." With that, he stormed out of the meeting room.

"I'll expect you to have your things out of the building by the end of the day," Striker called after him. "And security will be checking to make sure you don't do or take anything that you shouldn't."

Striker turned to face the rest of the executives. "Anyone else feel they want to jump ship?"

Instead of looking at him with fear, as if worried that they might be the next ones tossed out, everyone seated at the large conference table just grinned with relief. Striker knew from speaking to them all individually beforehand that Charles was the one rotten apple in the bunch.

"No? Good," Striker said with a smile of his own. "Because everyone else at this table has been willing to work with me. We are a team, folks. Working together we can make this place something special. As for Charles's vacancy, it will be filled effective immediately by Anna Sanchez, the assistant vice president of finance. As many of you know, Anna has trained the last three V.P.'s of finance during her ten years here. She's more than qualified to take on the responsibilities of this position."

"Thank you, Striker," Anna said.

After the meeting, Tex was waiting for him. "I heard about Charles. You know that if brains were gasoline, Charles couldn't run an ant's motorcycle."

"I take it you're not upset with my decision to accept Charles's resignation?"

"I'm happier than a coon in a cornfield."

"I'm glad to hear that, Tex."

"So how do you like your new office?" She nodded to the space next to Hank's old office.

After over a month of working in the cramped confines of the conference room where he'd first set up his ops H.Q., Striker had had to revise his plans and move into a bigger space. Using his grandfather's old office still didn't sit right with him, so he staked out his own territory in the office of a recently retired executive.

"It's fine."

"Don't knock me over with your enthusiasm now," Tex mocked him. "You Marines are such a rowdy bunch."

"It's nicer than a tick on a hound dog. How's that?"

"What's nice about a tick on a hound dog?" Tex countered. "If you're makin' up sayin's, then you need to do better than that."

"I'll work on it. In between all the other things I have to do."

Meanwhile, back at the ranch, his dad had yet to devise a practical solution to get on his mom's good side. Stan was still sleeping in the RV while Angela was in a guest bedroom. Striker had managed to avoid the sticky situation by spending more and more time at the office.

Kate dropped by occasionally that week but seemed determined to put some space between them. As long as Striker talked to her about his ideas for the company, she was an eager listener and indeed a creative thinker.

But whenever he attempted to turn the conversation to a more personal subject, she retreated. The only topic that was safe was their mutual confusion about their parents' behavior, which is what they talked about when Kate came by the following Monday morning.

"My mom is back home again but my father tells me she's not speaking to him."

"It's been eight days." He knew, because that's how long it had been since he'd kissed Kate. Had her mom said something to her to make Kate retreat? But it wasn't as if she'd totally retreated. She just wasn't kissing him. Obviously they had to get rid of this parental situation, then he'd figure out how to get Kate back into his arms. Without the worry of one of their parents interrupting them at a critical moment. "How long can they keep this up?"

"I guess we'll just have to wait and find out."

Striker didn't like that idea one bit. Waiting around was not a Marine's strong suit.

"Thanks for meeting me here," Jack told Stan Monday evening as they sat at a table in an upscale bar a few miles from Westwind. They both ordered beers—Stan's an American label, Jack's a German import.

"So," Jack began. "Is your wife still acting as crazy as mine is?"

"You mean not speaking to me?"

Jack nodded.

"Yeah." Stan took a healthy sip of his beverage. "How long do you think they're going to keep this up?"

"I have no idea. It's not logical."

"Agreed."

"I mean it's not like we committed some horrible crime. They are definitely overreacting in my opinion."

"Mine, too."

"I'm so glad you agree."

"So what do we do about it?" Stan demanded.

"Do?" Jack repeated.

"Yeah, *do*. We clearly have to take the offensive here. We can't just sit back and let them call the shots. It's time we launched a battle plan of our own."

"Well, you're the expert in battle plans," Jack countered. "What did you have in mind?"

"I may be an expert in battle plans, but I'm no expert when it comes to women. Which is why I called in reinforcements. Ah, there he is." Stan waved his hand. "Striker, over here!"

Striker had no idea that his dad would be joined by Jack Bradley when his dad had called asking Striker to meet him at this bar. "What's going on, guys?"

"We're having a planning session," Stan replied.

"Planning for what?"

"For the end to hostilities with the women in our lives."

"And you called me here because…?"

"Because you're the expert in the female department."

"What gives you that idea?" Striker countered.

"You haven't had any trouble with them in the past."

"Says who?"

Stan frowned. "You've never told me you had any trouble."

"Yeah, right." Striker laughed. "Like I'm going to tell my dad about my trouble with women."

"You mean you don't have any ideas on how to help us?" Jack said.

Striker placed his order for a bottle of Mexican beer before replying. "Have you tried apologizing?"

"For what?" Stan said. "We didn't do anything wrong."

"Well, right there you have a problem to begin with," Striker said. "The two of you did go a little overboard that night at the restaurant."

"Okay, so we may have overdone the competitive thing a little…"

"A *lot*."

"…but that's hardly something to get so upset over," Stan continued.

"Your women think so."

"What does Kate think?" Jack asked Striker.

"Who can figure out what Kate thinks?" Striker's expression turned brooding.

Just when he thought he was starting to figure her out, she sent him new conflicting messages. She'd been a surprising flirt when she'd caught him naked at the swimming hole and had delighted him with her comments and her kisses. But now she'd retreated back into her Ice Queen role.

Not really. While it was true that she'd pulled away some, she hadn't reverted back to her old self. Instead she was somewhere in between.

The question was why? Why was she keeping her distance? He could have sworn that she'd enjoyed their time together and their kisses as much as he did.

As much as Striker wanted her back in his arms, he sensed that this wasn't the time to pressure her. But that's all he'd figured out. Her reasons for needing more space were a complete mystery to him.

"Yeah. Women," Stan said. "Who knows what any of them think?"

Jack nodded and then shook his head. "Women."

Striker raised his bottle of Mexican beer for a toast. "To the females of the world."

"Let's be a little more specific," Jack suggested.

"To the females in our lives," Striker amended. "Inscrutable."

"Impossible," Stan added.

"Indispensable," Jack said.

They all took a drink, lost in their own thoughts.

"We were talking about problem solving at a management meeting at King Oil today," Striker noted. "I'm working on getting them to think the Marine Corps way. Team building. Creative ways to accomplish successful missions. Like the Crucible Event."

"What's that?" Jack asked.

"It's the culmination of basic training. The recruits are faced with a series of events that require they work together or fail."

"How does that apply to our predicament with the women in our lives?" Jack asked.

"Different ways of looking at a problem. Pooling re-

sources. Working together. I was thinking…maybe you
should borrow each other's strengths.''

''In what way?''

''Dad, you could pick up some of Jack's smooth
ways. Jack, how do you usually make amends with your
wife?''

''Flowers usually work. Not this time however.''

''Dad, when was the last time you gave Mom flowers?''

Stan got defensive. ''What is this, a test? I don't know
how long it's been.''

''If you can't remember, then it's been too long,''
Jack inserted.

''Okay, Dad, what's your strength? Jeez, this feels
more than a little weird,'' Striker had to confess with a
laugh. ''I'm not sure I want to know how my parents
make up after an argument.''

''Like I'm going to give you any juicy details,'' Stan
scoffed. ''A gentleman never kisses and tells.''

Striker returned his attention to Jack. ''You said that
flowers weren't working for you this time, right? Well,
then maybe you should try something different.''

''You mean like have my secretary order my wife
chocolate or jewelry instead of flowers?''

''I mean like taking action. And this is something
you'd have to do yourself, Jack. Not delegate to others.''

''Sweep her off her feet, man,'' Stan ordered Jack.
''Don't be a wimp about it!''

''Who are you calling a wimp?'' Jack glared at him.
''Angela is just as angry at you as Elizabeth is at me. I
don't see you making any headway.''

''Okay,'' Striker said. ''Let's not argue amongst our-
selves here. The team has to stay strong to be successful.
Let's have another toast.'' All three men lifted their
beers. ''To successful missions all around.''

Chapter Ten

"What did you do?" Kate demanded when she walked into Striker's office the next morning.

"Why?" he countered. "What went wrong?"

"Aha. I knew it. My dad told me that he met with you and your dad last night and that's why he and my mom have made up."

"Disclosing that could be grounds for court-martialing," Striker muttered.

"I would have loved to have been present at that planning session," Kate noted with a grin. "What did you guys talk about?"

"Women."

"What about them?"

"I can't disclose that without endangering the success of our mission."

"Which is?"

"To cease hostilities with the women in our lives."

Kate wondered if Striker was counting her as the woman in his life. She'd tried to take time-out and regain her perspective. But she'd missed him. Terribly.

And the time they'd been apart had not made her want him any less. Quite the opposite.

She was surprised that he hadn't pressed her, that he hadn't tried to turn their conversations into more personal territory. But she was also grateful that he'd given her the time to think.

Even so, she wasn't quite ready to talk to Striker about her feelings yet, so she returned to the safer topic of their parents.

"Well, whatever you did, it worked. What about your folks? Have they kissed and made up?"

"Apparently, since my dad finally slept in the house last night."

"Does that mean your father has accepted your coming here to run King Oil?"

"I don't know if I'd go that far. He's stopped hassling me about it for the time being."

"That's good, right?"

"Yeah. I get hassled enough by Charles. Or I did until he resigned yesterday. He doesn't approve of my roughshod methods. And he never did understand the concept of pulling together."

"Then it's a good thing that he's gone."

"I wasn't expecting to hear you say that," Striker admitted.

"Why not?"

"I don't know. Maybe because Charles was an establishment kind of guy."

"What's that supposed to mean?"

"That he fits into the corporate environment."

"Yet you fired him."

"I accepted his resignation."

"What makes you think that he fits the corporate environment more than you do?"

"I didn't say that."

"You didn't have to. During the time you've been in charge of King Oil, you've shaken things up, made changes that are good for the company and its employees."

"That's the first time you've told me that."

"You're a natural leader, Striker. Surely you know that. And as you're always telling me, leading Marines isn't that different from leading civilians."

"Except that Marines are much better at accepting orders."

"Even so, you've done a great job here. You've motivated people to come up with new ways of doing things. You've got them fired up about working here."

"And you know all this how?"

"From talking to Tex and some of the other people involved."

"Checking up on me behind my back?"

"There's the Force Recon Marine in you coming out again. Not trusting anyone. When are you going to see me as someone on your side? On your team?"

"When are you going to kiss me again?" The words were out of Striker's mouth before he could recall them.

Smooth, real smooth. "Never mind. I shouldn't have said that. This isn't the proper place to discuss personal issues."

"I agree."

Her voice sounded cool again, and she sure was looking all buttoned up and proper. The suit she wore today was dark blue. She was seated across from him and had crossed her legs at the knee, which made her skirt hike up. He'd been stealing appreciative looks throughout their conversation. And, yeah, her hair was loose today, but it was smooth instead of all mussed up as it was after he kissed her.

The desire to reach out and mess up her perfect hair

with his hands, to smudge her flawless lipstick with his mouth, was almost overwhelming.

His thoughts froze and his body hardened.

It took all his self-control to act as if he weren't burning up inside and to instead remain calm.

"So why don't we continue this conversation tonight? At my place," Kate said. "Over dinner."

"What?" He couldn't have heard her correctly.

"I said, why don't we continue this conversation tonight over dinner."

"You mean our conversation about King Oil?"

"No."

"About our parents?"

"No. About us. What do you say?"

He was just about speechless. But he quickly recovered. "Fine. What time?"

"Is seven all right with you?"

Striker nodded.

"Good. I'll see you then."

He could have sworn she positively sashayed out the door. The sway of her hips packed the punch of a grenade launcher.

He blinked at the realization that Tex was standing before him, waving her hand across his bemused face. "I'm trustin' that you are not AWOL."

"Absent without leave?"

"A wolf on the loose."

Striker stared down at the bouquet of flowers in his hand and wondered if he'd lost his mind. What was he doing standing here, waiting outside Kate's door like some nervous recruit?

He was part of the Marine Corps's most elite fighting force—a Force Recon Marine. He could accomplish ambitious assaults with one hand tied behind his back. He was a master at behind-the-lines infiltration. He'd seen the good, the bad and the ugly in this world.

He wasn't a man who believed in dreams. He wasn't a man who dwelled on nightmares. He was a man who lived in the present because that's the only thing that was a sure bet. The here and now.

So why was he hesitating? Why was he second-guessing himself?

Well, for one thing, he had a feeling that Kate wanted to talk about their relationship and it was natural for a guy to be leery of that. Any conversation with a female that began with the words "We have to talk" was greeted by a guy with about as much enthusiasm as an enema.

But Kate wasn't like most women. She was unique. Just when he thought he was breaking the code, she changed it. Not that she was deliberately trying to be a tease. He didn't think that was the case here.

She was a challenge. She kept him on his toes. She surprised him again and again. She made him want her more and more.

Which brought him back to the reason he was standing there like a sap, with a bunch of fancy flowers in his hand.

He knew that she wasn't keen on hooking up with a Marine. So maybe he should back off right now, before things got even more serious than they were.

He didn't know. He'd never thought long-term before.

He only knew he wanted to be with her, wanted her in his arms, wanted her lips beneath his. And he also knew it was more than just lust at work here. There was something else...

But being a guy, he wasn't real eager to put a label on it.

His mom had already given him the third degree when

she'd stopped by King Oil earlier in the day. She'd also told him that her time in Texas was over, that it was time for her to move on. She'd made her peace with Striker's dad, and with her own father, visiting the cemetery to pay her last respects.

But before she'd left, she'd grilled Striker about Kate. She'd ended the conversation saying, "I would like to have grandkids before I get too old to enjoy them. Which means you'd have to get married first."

Married? To Kate? The image wasn't as scary as it should have been.

Enough. This was getting him nowhere. He needed to take action. His knock on her door was loud enough to qualify as a pounding.

The second Kate opened the door and Striker stepped inside, he shoved the flowers at her with one hand while tugging her into his arms with the other.

Two thoughts hit him. 1) That she was where she belonged. 2) He was glad he hadn't bought her roses or the thorns would be digging into both of them as they kissed.

Kate vaguely knew that some sort of floral arrangement was being crushed between them. She could smell carnations as she tasted Striker's passion. The tangled web of passion enveloped her as surely as his arms enveloped her. His kiss evoked an intimacy that was both sensuous and tender. He'd claimed her mouth as if it were the cup of life to be drained to the end.

The passion built as one kiss blended into another, his tongue mating with hers. He was a master of the endless kiss. This was no teasing flirtation. This was total possession. His kiss became hotter, deeper, sweeter.

Fireworks, bells ringing, alarms going off...

Wait, that was a *real* alarm. Her smoke alarm. Her dinner!

Kate pulled away and rushed into the kitchen where smoke was bellowing from the grill where she'd had two steaks cooking. They were now charred beyond recognition.

"I like my meat well-done," Striker drawled, "but not quite that well-done."

She turned on him. "This is your fault. You distracted me."

"Is that all I was doing?"

He was giving her that look again. And using that seductive tone of voice. He'd done a lot more than distract her. He'd stolen her heart.

The sound of her stomach growling with unladylike intensity interrupted her soul-searching.

"I need food," she muttered. "And I need it fast." She reached for the phone book. "Do you want Mexican, Thai or Chinese takeout?"

"Chinese sounds fine."

Half an hour later they were sitting on a sheepskin rug on either side of the weathered pine coffee table in her living room, dipping chopsticks into various cartons of food. Or, to be more precise, Striker was dipping, she was stabbing. Kate was no pro where chopsticks were concerned.

"Where did you learn to use these so well?" She waggled the chopsticks at him.

"Why? Are you impressed with my manual dexterity?"

"Mmm." She already knew he had the ability to undo her bra in the blink of an eye, despite the fact that a tornado whirled over their heads.

"Shall I show you what else I can do with my hands?"

"Shall I show you what I can do with mine?" she countered, loving playing the seductress with him. It wasn't a role she'd ever had the confidence to attempt before.

"Oh yeah."

"Are you ready?"

"Oh yeah."

"Are you sure?"

"If I were any more ready I'd explode."

"We can't have that." She scooted around the edge of the coffee table so that she was beside him. Then she ran the tips of her fingers over his jawline, slightly rough with stubble. "Are you watching?" She trailed one hand down his shirtfront, playing with the buttons on his denim shirt but not undoing them. Every so often she'd dart her finger between the material to caress his bare chest.

"I'm watching…and waiting."

She could feel the rumble of his voice beneath her hand.

"Are you in a hurry?"

"Depends what you have in mind."

"Telling you that would ruin the anticipation, now wouldn't it?"

Her hand lowered to his abdomen. She swirled the tip of her nail around his navel before leaning closer to daintily lick the corner of his mouth. "Mmm, you taste good."

"So do you…" He lightly brushed his lips across hers, barely touching yet arousing intense emotions.

She pulled back. The last time they'd kissed the smoke alarm had gone off. While in his embrace, she'd lost track of time, of everything. "We really do need to talk…."

Striker groaned. "Later." He murmured the words against her mouth.

"No." She leaned away. If he kissed her again she

wouldn't be able to think at all. "Now. We have to talk now."

"Are you having second thoughts because we work together?"

She nodded. That was one of the reasons. And there was still the fact that he was a Marine. But he'd changed since coming to King Oil. She'd seen the transformation since he'd suggested starting with a clean slate.

"So what do you suggest we do?"

She hadn't expected him to put the ball in her court. She'd expected him to take charge, as he so often did.

"I thought we could talk about that."

"Start by telling me why you backed off this past week," Striker demanded. "Was it something your mother said to you?"

"No. What made you think that?"

"You haven't been the same since she caught us kissing outside your loft that night."

"It wasn't anything she said."

"Then what was it?"

"I needed time to think."

He reached out to cup her cheek in the palm of his hand. "Just don't tell me that you want to end this."

"I don't. Can we just take things one day at a time and see where that leads us?"

"I think I can manage that if you can."

"I can." She just didn't know if she could manage not falling in love with him. She had a feeling it was already too late.

The next few weeks went by in a blur of happiness. Kate had no idea that taking each day as it came and enjoying the moment could be so wonderful. The October sun seemed brighter, the air clearer. She smiled more often and laughed a lot. And she relaxed.

On days when Kate didn't have a court appearance, she'd replace her power suit with a stylish look like the beige suede skirt and black jersey top she wore today. She'd brought lunch from her favorite deli to Striker's office. They were seated on a red-and-white gingham tablecloth that she'd packed in her oversized tote bag.

"What else do you have in there?" Striker asked. "Any dessert?"

"You'll just have to wait and see."

It didn't matter how many times she'd seen him in jeans and a denim shirt, he never failed to make her heart race. He looked so completely at home, surrounded by financial spreadsheets and management reports. His short hair had gotten a little longer, his tan a little deeper. She could just sit there and watch him forever.

Looking up, he grinned at her. Again, she noticed how that changed his entire face. The dark side of him that she'd noticed when they'd first met had melted into the background, allowing the more fun-loving Striker to come out. The one who loved his collection of Hawaiian shirts, who sang along with country-western songs on the radio.

"I'm driving down to the coast for another set of meetings with the guys on the oil rigs in the Gulf on Friday," he said. "Want to join me?"

"To visit an oil rig?"

"You can lie on the beach while I do that."

"Is that your way of saying you'd like to see me in a swimsuit?"

His grin deepened. "Absolutely. Was I that obvious?"

"No, you were quite smooth."

"So, will you come with me? It's not that long a drive. A few hours. We don't have to stay overnight if you don't want to."

Oh, but she did want to. Intensely.

"King Oil has a corporate beach house down there, right on the Gulf. It's got several bedrooms."

We'll only need one. She didn't speak the words aloud but they resonated in her heart. The time had come.

"Yes, I'll come with you."

"Great."

And it was great. The weather was perfect when he picked her up on Friday morning. The drive down was scenic or maybe it was just her state of mind. Everything looked good to her, from road signs to the silhouette of live oak.

It had taken her several hours to decide what to wear, but now she was glad she'd gone with the black denim skirt and the red off-the-shoulder top. The skirt was shorter than those Striker had previously seen her in, and his heated gaze told her he approved. She'd packed enough clothes for a week, and not one single business suit. She'd packed two swimsuits. The first was a traditional one-piece, the other was a bikini that showed more skin than she'd ever displayed before. She still wasn't sure if she'd have the nerve to wear it.

But she was sure that she wanted to be with Striker. He looked great as always in his jeans and denim shirt.

"Tell me something about yourself," she said. "Something most people don't know about you."

"That I know the lyrics to Kenny Rogers's 'The Gambler.'"

She laughed. "I know that already. I've heard you sing it. Tell me something else. Tell me about your name. It's an unusual one. At first I thought it might be a nickname, but it's on your birth certificate." She knew because that document was in the file she had on him regarding his inheritance.

"My mom usually loves telling this story and she does a much better job of it than I do."

"She's not here now." His parents had continued their travels in the RV. "So you tell me."

"It was a dark and stormy night…"

"It always is in stories like this."

"My mom was pregnant with me. My dad was stationed at Camp Pendleton in San Diego. I wasn't due for another three weeks. So my dad saw no harm in driving her up along the coast when she insisted on getting away from the congestion of the city. They got off the main highway and took a few detours. Then I decided to come early. My dad probably could have managed a normal delivery but there was a complication. Things were getting dicey when another car finally came along. As fate would have it, the driver was a country doctor. An older guy, but he knew what to do. Saved my life and my mother's. In gratitude, my father promised to name his newborn son after the doctor. When he discovered the doctor's name was Otis Striker, he went with the Striker part. For which I am eternally grateful. Growing up with a name like Otis would have been tough."

"What about your brothers? Do they have unusual names, too?" She'd seen their names in the file but hadn't paid much attention.

"Not all of them, no. My youngest brothers are twins, but you probably already knew that."

She did remember Hank talking about the twins.

"What about you?" Striker reached over to twine his fingers through hers. "Tell me something about you that most people don't know."

"That I love the Dixie Chicks song 'Cowboy Take Me Away.'"

"What else?"

"That Halloween is my least favorite holiday."

"I don't know… I seem to recall enjoying your hand-ing out goodies the other night."

Striker had come to her loft with a stack of scary videos and a pizza. He'd clearly gotten a kick out of watching the few kids who'd come to her door. He'd taken even more pleasure in hand-feeding her slices of pizza and kissing the tomato sauce from her lips.

"So what do you have against Halloween?"

"Perhaps I should have said that Halloween used to be my least favorite holiday. You changed that last night."

"Glad to hear it."

Striker had changed a lot of things for her. She'd stopped worrying about the future. She'd stopped being so uptight about perfection. He was driving an Ameri-can-made convertible and the wind was messing up her hair. She didn't care. She was with Striker and that was enough.

They arrived at Port Aransas by noon, passing motel courts, bait shops and beach cottages until they reached their destination. Located right on the edge of the broad, gently sloping beach was the stunning house.

The floor plan was an open concept; the living area blended with the kitchen, and the focus was on the view through the huge windows. The master bedroom was on the main floor, and the guest bedrooms upstairs.

Striker opened the sliding door that led to the deck facing the Gulf. He inhaled the salt air. "This reminds me of my beach house on Pirate's Cove. A little island off the coast of North Carolina. It's not as grand as this place. It's an A-frame and I helped build it. But it's all mine. Anyway, I'll let you settle in while I head out to my meeting. I should be back by four."

"Come on, admit it, you're getting a kick out of this," she said.

"Out of being here with you?"

"Out of running King Oil."

"I guess I am." He kissed her quickly and headed out.

Kate wasn't sure how to unpack given the fact that she wanted to share the master bedroom with Striker tonight. Be bold, she told herself. So she hung her clothes in the closet. And unpacked the few things that Striker had brought with him, including two of his beloved Hawaiian shirts.

And because she was a bold woman now, she also decided to put on the black bikini she'd brought instead of the one-piece swimsuit. After applying sunscreen, she sat out on the deck and enjoyed the sun and the surf. She hadn't brought any work with her—a first for her. So she amused herself by watching the sandpipers skittering along the water, staying just ahead of the rolling surf. Pelicans patrolled the skies, hunting fish in the shallow water. This section of the beach was quiet this time of year.

She must have dozed off, because the next time she glanced at her watch it was almost four. She went inside to freshen up in preparation for Striker's return when she heard a noise from the master bedroom.

"Is that you, Striker?"

"Yeah."

"I didn't know you were back. You should have come out and gotten me…"

She paused on the threshold to the master bedroom. Striker was rapidly returning his clothing to his bag. Was this his way of telling her he didn't want to share a bedroom with her?

Don't panic, she ordered herself. Find out what's going on. Ask him. Don't assume the worst.

"Did something happen at the meeting? Do we have to go back to San Antonio?"

"Yeah. I've got a plane to catch."

"A plane? Where to?"

"Washington. The Marine Corps needs me."

Chapter Eleven

"The Marine Corps?" Kate couldn't believe this was happening. Maybe she'd fallen asleep out on the deck and this was just a nightmare. Maybe if she pinched herself she'd wake up...

It didn't work. Striker still stood there packing.

She tried to draw air into her lungs, but it suddenly seemed too heavy to breathe. The tightness in her chest intensified at his remote expression.

"That's right. The Marine Corps."

"I don't understand." Her brain refused to cooperate, unable to process what she was hearing. A desperate chill set in. She grabbed the brightly colored cotton wrap she'd left on the bed and awkwardly slid her arms into the sleeves before wrapping it around her. The trembling that had begun within her heart had now spread throughout her entire body.

Today was supposed to be the moment, the time when she and Striker shared the ultimate intimacy and made love. Instead he stood there, telling her that the Marine

Corps needed him. What about her? She needed him, too.

"My two-month deployment here is over. I'm needed on a special op overseas."

"Your deployment?" That certainly put it into perspective. Pain tightened her throat, making it hard for her to get the words out. "Is that all this was for you? Another mission?"

"I thought you understood."

"Well, I don't! I thought you wanted to continue on here at King Oil."

"And I thought you'd accepted me as I am. A Force Recon Marine."

"You never talked about returning to the Marines."

"What was there to talk about?"

"The fact that you had no intention of staying here. That what we had together was nothing more than another fling for you."

"You never talked about what would happen at the end of the two months, either."

He was right. She'd avoided the subject, even though she knew the date was rapidly arriving, had in fact arrived. Today. She'd told herself it was because she was trusting in the future, not anticipating the worst. She'd been foolish to stick her head in the sand.

"How long have you known?"

"I got the message an hour ago."

"And you couldn't wait to get back here and pack your bags." She was overcome with déjà vu of Ted's eagerness to head off to some new and dangerous adventure. And now here was Striker, doing exactly the same thing.

"I never lied to you."

"You never told me the truth, either." He'd let her believe that he might be staying indefinitely at King Oil.

Had let her fall in love with him. "Because you knew that if you told me you were returning to the Marines that I wouldn't get involved with you."

Her accusation scored a direct hit with Striker. She was right. He hadn't been completely upfront with her.

Striker knew he should have avoided getting involved with Kate. But he couldn't help himself. A first for him. Usually his self-discipline was immense. But not where Kate was concerned.

Even so, a part of him had hoped that she'd cared for him enough to honor his commitment to the Marine Corps, to understand his duty. To say she'd wait for him. That clearly wasn't the case.

"This seems to be where I came in." His jaw clenched. "With you saying how much you dislike Marines. It was fine when you pretended I was the head of King Oil, wasn't it? Then it was great for me to kiss you. It was fine for you to flirt with me. To hang your clothes next to mine in the closet."

So he had noticed. "I thought we had a future together," she shot back, blinking away the tears.

"So did I. But clearly you want something I can't give you. You want someone I'm not." His expression was dark and closed in, shutting her out. "I've got a plane to catch." He placed the car keys on the dresser. "You're welcome to use my car to go back to San Antonio."

He was gone a second later, leaving her standing there all alone, her dreams shattered by reality once again.

Two days later, Kate was curled up on her couch, screening her calls through her answering machine. "Kate, this is your mother. Pick up the phone. I know you're there. I'm downstairs, right outside your building and I'll be up there in two minutes."

Great. That's all she needed. Her mother telling her what a mess Kate had made of her life.

Kate lifted the receiver. "There's no need for you to come over."

"There certainly is. Your father told me that you stayed home from the office yesterday and today."

"It's the flu."

"It's the Marine. I heard Striker has left town. I'm standing outside your door. Let me in."

Kate reluctantly did, but only because she knew her mother wouldn't go away. "I know, I know. I look awful, right?" Her eyes were red and so was her nose. She'd never been a pretty crier.

"Oh, honey." Elizabeth patted her shoulder awkwardly. "You look like a woman who's had her heart broken."

Kate wiped away the tears. "It's my own fault."

"I find that hard to believe."

"It's true." Kate curled up on her couch again. "Striker told me from the very beginning how important the Marine Corps is to him. It's as much a part of him as his green eyes. But I thought I could change him, that being at King Oil would turn him into something he's not."

"You're not the first woman who thought she could change a man."

"Then he wouldn't be Striker." That realization had hit her about an hour after he'd left. He wasn't like Ted. He wasn't returning to the Marine Corps for the mere thrill of it. He was doing so out of a sense of duty. She got it now. "He's following his dream."

"What about your dreams?"

"Exactly. I haven't been sitting here these two days feeling sorry for myself. Well, maybe I was, a little...that first day. But not anymore."

"Then why are you still crying?"

"Because I'm sorry it took me so long to understand. The silver lining is that I've reached some decisions about my life."

Elizabeth sat down beside her and patted her hand. "Good for you."

Kate wasn't sure her mother would still think so after hearing what she had in mind. But that didn't change her determination any.

She was going to do what had to be done. What she should have done years ago. It had taken a catalyst like Striker to make her reexamine her life and the choices she'd made. "I used to think that things happen for a reason. Especially bad things. And that reason was because of me."

"You?" Elizabeth frowned. "I don't understand. What do you mean?"

"You remember when Grandma died?"

Elizabeth nodded.

"Remember how I didn't want to go see her? A few days later she was dead."

"You thought that was your fault?"

"I felt guilty, yes. And guilt has prevented me from following my dreams."

"Guilt about your grandmother's death?"

"And more. About Ted."

"Your grandmother had a stroke and Ted died in a car accident. You had nothing to do with either of those occurrences."

"I didn't want to marry Ted." It was the first time she'd told her mother that. "The closer we got to the wedding, the more I fantasized about running away. I was thinking about leaving him that day...the day he was killed." She didn't tell her mom about the crush

CATHIE LINZ 171

she'd had on Striker. There was only so much she could share.

But if Kate didn't come completely clean, she couldn't start fresh. As difficult as it was, she had to dump the ugly baggage once and for all.

"There's more. I've never told anyone this…" Kate's gaze pleaded with her mother to understand. She was taking a big emotional risk here. But that's something the new Kate had vowed to do. Not to let fear or guilt paralyze her any longer. "I had a crush on Striker. I'd seen him a couple times that summer when he was nineteen and came to Hank's ranch. He didn't notice me at all, but I daydreamed about him a lot during that time."

"Oh, honey."

"I know you probably think that makes me a bad person…"

"I think it makes you human. You think I never experienced guilt? What about when your grandmother died? You said you felt guilty but I was the one who made the decision not to visit her. She was my mother, I should have known something was wrong, should have gone to visit her. But I didn't. And that's not the only time… When I was in competitions, there was one time when I was sixteen when I badly wanted to win. Well, I always wanted to win, but this was for Miss Junior Austin. There was one girl who was prettier and more accomplished than I was. She was all that I thought stood between me and that title. So I actually hoped that something bad would happen to her. It did. She had appendicitis. It ruptured and she had to be rushed to the hospital. She almost died. I felt like I'd done that to her." Elizabeth paused to face Kate. "You do know that we don't have that kind of power, right? That the power is actually in the guilt, which stays with you like a burr under your skin. It made me want a perfect life, where nothing was wrong. If nothing went wrong, then I wouldn't have anything else to feel guilty about.''

"You never said anything.''

"Of course not. Saying it would mean acknowledging the guilt. I thought if I didn't talk about it that it would go away. Only it never did.''

"I know.'' Kate could sure relate to that. "I was getting ready to tell you and Dad that I wanted to leave the family firm and go into public law when Dad had his heart attack two years ago. Again, guilt held me back. Because by then this pattern had developed. Whenever I tried to do what I wanted, instead of what was expected of me, bad things happened. People died. Or almost died.''

"I had no idea you felt this way. Why didn't you ever tell me any of this before? Silly question. We never had that kind of relationship, did we?'' Elizabeth's voice was filled with regret. "I was one of the reasons you were doing things that made you miserable. You were doing them to make your father and me happy.''

"It's not your fault. I'm an adult. I made my own choices.''

"Under the pressure of expectations from your father and I.''

"I'm not doing that anymore. I can't. After that disastrous dinner that night on the River Walk, Striker talked about living the life you wanted instead of the one that was expected of you. I need to do that now. I need to live the life I want.''

"What does that mean?''

"That I want to work for Children's Services as an advocate for kids and families in need.''

"What about Striker?''

"He was right. About some things. But he was wrong when he said that I wanted someone he's not. I don't. I want him. Just the way he is. I guess I needed shaking out of my sheltered little world to realize what I was missing. I was missing having my own life. I was missing love. By playing it safe, I wasn't really *playing* at all. I was just a spectator. Well, not anymore. I've finally come to terms with my past. And that's given me the courage to see a new future for myself. I love you and Dad, but I can't keep living the life you want me to. I have to follow my own dreams.''

''I guess I knew this day was coming.'' Elizabeth took a steadying breath and surreptitiously wiped away a tear. ''Babs will be most upset that you're not hooking up with Rodney, you know.'' She laughed at Kate's expression. ''Relax, I was just teasing. I guess you and I have both had a few moments of self-discovery recently.'' She looked at Kate uncertainly before slowly holding out her arms. ''How about a hug?''

The two women embraced before breaking away with nervous laughter and tears.

Elizabeth quickly wiped away the moisture from her cheeks. ''Now, let's break out some champagne. The last time I was here I saw that you hadn't opened the bottle we gave you for New Year's. We need to celebrate.''

''I still have to tell Dad my decision. I don't know how he's going to take the news.''

''Leave your father to me. You just worry about that new life of yours.''

Three weeks later, Striker had just completed his debriefing at the Marine Corps headquarters in Quantico regarding his latest special op mission and was about to leave the building when he was handed a message. *Urgent, please call immediately.*

The number was his parents' cell phone.

His stomach clenched but his fingers were steady as

he quickly punched the memory button on his own cell phone. His mom answered on the first ring.

"It's Striker. What's wrong? Is it Dad?"

"No, your father is fine. So are your brothers. It's Kate."

"Did she call you? Why? To try and get you to convince me to go back to King Oil?"

"Striker, shut up and listen. There's been an accident. Elizabeth called to tell me. Kate was in a car accident. She's in critical condition."

Fear skidded through his body and slammed into his heart. He'd always been the one who lived with danger. He'd never once considered the idea that something might happen to Kate.

His years of military training was the only thing preventing him from panicking. Even so, his voice was rough with emotion. "Give me the name of the hospital in San Antonio and I'll catch the next flight down there." He had some liberty time coming after this last mission.

"She's not in San Antonio. She's in Washington. Or in Virginia to be exact." She gave him the name of the hospital. "Her parents are there already. The accident happened last night. They flew in first thing this morning. Striker, Kate hasn't regained consciousness. It's not looking good."

"I'm on my way."

Striker made the drive in record time and he entered the hospital at a run. The mantra *Let her be okay, let her be okay,* ran through his head even as he stopped by the front desk for more information. The woman there seemed to take forever to tell him what room Kate was in and how to get there.

He saw her parents the second he stepped out of the elevator. They looked as devastated as he felt. Not that it showed. He had his war face on. The one that got things done. The one that won battles.

Elizabeth greeted him with a wobbly smile. "Striker, I'm so glad you're here."

"I just got back. What's her condition? What do the doctors say?"

"Her condition hasn't changed," Jack replied. "She hasn't regained consciousness. The doctors tell us the next twenty-four hours will be critical. They don't know if she's going to make it." His voice broke.

"Of course she's going to make it." Striker's voice was rock solid even though his gut clenched.

"She came to Washington to see you," Elizabeth said. "Your mom told her that you were coming back and she wanted to see you."

Guilt slammed into him.

As if reading his thoughts, Elizabeth immediately placed her hand on his arm. "No, don't do that. No guilt. Kate wouldn't want that. She came here of her own free will. She's made some changes since you've been gone. Major changes. She's gone to work for Children's Services as an advocate for kids and families in need."

Striker remembered Kate talking about doing something like that, but he never really believed she'd be willing to give up her high-paying job with her family's law firm. Now he realized how badly he'd misjudged her. And how much he loved her.

He'd known he'd missed her. He'd known he'd thought about her while overseas. He'd known then that his feelings ran deep, and were the permanent kind.

If only he'd told her. If only he'd said something before leaving her in Texas. Then she wouldn't have come to Washington, wouldn't have been in the car accident.

"She loves working for Children's Services. It's

something she's always wanted to do," Elizabeth was saying. "But guilt held her back."

"Guilt?" He didn't understand.

Elizabeth briefly filled him in, from Kate's guilt about her grandmother's death to her guilt about her father's heart attack. "She really thought that following her dreams resulted in other people paying the price with their lives. And now here she is following her dream and *she's* the one hurt, fighting for her life." Tears ran down her face. "The doctors didn't seem hopeful."

When Jack placed his arm around her, she buried her face in his shoulder.

Striker refused to accept the grim medical prognosis. "The doctors are wrong. She's going to make it. I'm not giving up on her," he said fiercely. "And you can't, either. Do you hear me? I am *not* letting her go."

Chapter Twelve

Striker entered Kate's hospital room, prepared for the worst. Even so, seeing her lying there, so pale and still, hooked up to monitors and IVs, was almost more than he could bear. The sound of the machinery was surreal, the beeps mingling with his thundering heartbeat.

He was by her side an instant later.

"It's Striker." He took her hand in his. "I'm here, Kate. And I'm not leaving. You can't leave, either, Kate. There are people here who love you. You are *not* going to die on me, do you hear me? Do not die. That's an order."

At first Striker's voice was commanding, as if he could make her regain consciousness through the sheer power of his will. Nurses came and went. One even tried to tell him visiting hours were over, but one look at his fierce face and she backed down. And through it all he held Kate's hand and talked to her.

Darkness fell. Jack joined him at her bedside. "You need to go eat. I'll take over—"

"I'm not moving." Striker's intense gaze remained fixed on Kate.

A few hours later, Elizabeth placed her hand on his shoulder. "Striker, you've been sitting here since this morning. You need a break."

"I'm not leaving her."

"You can't be sure that she can even hear you."

"I am sure. And I'm not leaving."

He saw the tears in Elizabeth's eyes, saw the hopeless despair growing on her face as she turned away.

Striker refused to give in to the desperation churning in his gut. It was hard. One of the hardest things he'd ever had to do, and there had been many. Too many. So much despair in the world, so much evil, so much brutality too often at the expense of those least able to protect themselves.

The last hospital Striker had visited had been at a refugee camp in Afghanistan. Women and children scrambling to stay alive in a fierce environment. Memories that had to be packaged up and put on the shelf. Easy to say. Hard to do. Necessary. Or you risked giving in to the nightmares. Surrendering to the darkness.

You got on with the job. You completed the mission. Plan, prepare, execute.

No, he would not surrender. He would not give in to the desperation clawing to get out. You ordered it into oblivion. You willed it away. You kept going.

Striker talked until his voice grew hoarse. He told Kate stories about his childhood, about his brothers. He reminded her of their time together, of the drunken brawl at the barbecue, of the tornado, of Midnight's jealousy.

He even sang Kenny Rogers's "The Gambler" for

her. He told her jokes. He read to her. He made up Texas sayings.

He watched her face for any change, any sign that she was hearing him. But there was nothing. Her hand remained limp in his, her eyes closed.

Yet still he talked.

As time went on, as the darkest hours of the night dragged on, his orders became entreaties. "Come back to me, Kate. Don't leave me. You can't leave me. I need you. I need to see your smile, to hear your voice. I need you more than I need air, Kate." His voice, a hoarse whisper, cracked. "I didn't get it before, but I understand now." Pain resonated in every ragged breath he took. "I love you." He bowed his proud head over her hand. "I love you."

Striker, the warrior able to fight so many enemies, had finally run into something greater than himself. His love for Kate.

He was in danger of being pulled into the abyss of dwindling hope when he felt something. So weak at first that it felt like the flutter of a hummingbird's wings.

It took him a moment to realize that he wasn't imagining things. Kate *was* moving her fingers.

Looking up, he gazed into her eyes, those bluer-than-a-Texas-sky eyes. They were open. Kate had finally regained consciousness.

He raised her captured hand to his lips before pressing his face into her palm. Then he lifted tormented eyes to her. "I love you, Kate. I love you, I love you, I love you." He kept repeating the words, as if saying them would keep her with him.

Kate heard him. Even when the gray mist had held her in its swirling depths, she'd heard him. Been aware of his hand holding hers, caressing her fingers, willing her to return to him. But the pain had been intense. And a bright light had beckoned.

She'd resisted. Because there had always been Striker's voice, his presence, his will. Begging her to come back to him.

Her vision cleared and she saw him at her bedside. The bearded stubble on his face...the agony in his red-rimmed eyes...the slight dampness on his cheeks.

She'd had to fight to come back...to find her Marine crying for her. The ultimate sacrifice on his part.

She shifted so that her fingers brushed his cheek. "I...love you, too." Her voice sounded rusty and un-even, but that didn't seem to matter to him.

His smile was the most beautiful thing she'd ever seen. "You came back to me."

"Of...course. As if I'd...disobey an order from...the man...the Marine that I love."

Striker stared down at the huge bouquet of flowers in his hand and remembered the last time he'd brought Kate flowers. He'd come to her loft when she'd wanted to talk.

And now here he was, flowers in hand again, with Kate wanting to talk. She'd told him so when he'd left the hospital last night.

It had been almost two days since she'd regained con-sciousness. The doctors said she'd make a complete re-covery now that she was out of danger and would be released from their care tomorrow.

And so she wanted to talk to him.

Old habits were hard to break, and the truth was that he was more than a little nervous as to what she might say. But knowing she loved him made a huge difference.

And that she was okay. Armed with those two facts, he could face anything.

"Are those for me?" Kate asked as he held out the beautiful bouquet.

"Absolutely." He carefully set the glass vase on the windowsill. He'd gotten the biggest bunch of flowers the hospital gift shop had to offer.

"That was sweet of you. Thank you."

"You're welcome."

"I think we really do need to talk, Striker."

His stomach sank.

"I don't know how to put this...." Kate continued nervously. "So I guess I'll just come out and say it. Sometimes people say things in the drama of a life-and-death situation that maybe they don't mean to say."

He felt sucker punched. "You mean when you told me you loved me?"

She frowned. "No, I mean when *you* told me you loved me."

"I knew exactly what I was saying. But you...you'd just regained consciousness. Maybe you were overcome by the emotion of the moment. If you have regrets..."

"No way." She reached for his hand and twined her fingers through his. "I'm the one who's had a crush on you since she was seventeen."

"What are you talking about?"

"You heard me. The first time I saw you, you were skinny-dipping at the pond. I hid in the bushes and watched you. And then fantasized about you for the rest of the summer. That's why my guilt about Ted was so intense. Because despite the fact that I got engaged to him, I was still having these fantasies about you."

"I wish I'd known."

"I used to hang around the barn just to get a chance to look at you."

"Wait a minute." His eyes narrowed. "You were that girl, the one I never got a good look at, who'd always stand just out of sight. You had a white cowboy hat and you'd talk to Tony a lot. That was you, wasn't it?"

She nodded.

"You never talked to me."

"I was too tongue-tied."

"I wish you'd told me sooner. So you really did mean it when you said you loved me? Because I sure meant it when I said I loved you. I can't imagine my life without you."

"I was trying to be noble and give you a chance to back out if you wanted...."

"There's *no* way I want to back out."

"I was going to wait until you got out of the hospital, but just so you don't get any more wild ideas..." He reached inside the pocket of his Hawaiian shirt to fish out...a ring! "Will you do me the honor of becoming my wife?"

She was speechless.

He was nervous.

"I know that my being a Marine is difficult for you." His voice was gruff. "That you think that I'm addicted to the thrill of danger. That may have been the case in the past, but seeing you lying on this hospital bed...well, suffice it to say that it made me rethink my priorities. I used to think I'd stay in the Marines forever, but now..." He swallowed. "Anyway, you don't have to give me an answer right away. Take all the time you want..."

"I don't want any time. I don't need it." She blinked

back tears. "The answer is yes. I'd be honored to be your wife."

"Ooh-rah!" He punched a fist in the air and his smile took her breath away. He took her hand in his and slid the diamond solitaire onto her ring finger. "You can trade it in for something else if you don't like it. I told the jeweler I wanted something classic and elegant, like you."

"It's beautiful."

"Then why are you crying?"

"Because I'm so happy. And because I love you so much. You, not the money. You, the man with so much honor and commitment to his beloved Marines, to the greater good." She cupped his face with her hand. "You're my *forever* love, my destiny." She tugged him onto the bed beside her.

"You've got that right," Striker murmured against her lips before kissing her with his heart and soul.

Six months later…

"You were clever, I'll give you that." Striker gazed down at the headstone with his grandfather's name engraved on it. He laid a small bouquet of bluebonnets on the grave. "You deliberately maneuvered things so they'd work out this way—with me interested in running King Oil." The powers that be had transferred Striker from active to reserve duty so that he could take over the reins at the company. Should his country need him, he was still on call. But there were other things in his life now. He no longer had to live on the edge to feel alive. He only had to look into Kate's eyes. "Sure, I leave the paperwork to others, but the vision of where the company is going and how it can get there is mine.

I'm enjoying it, I admit it. I've even moved into your old office, which is what you probably had in mind all along. And I'm marrying Kate. Was that in your plans as well? Probably. In which case, I owe you big-time." Striker paused a moment. "I'm sorry you're not here today to see us tie the knot. But I have a feeling you're up there looking down on us with a fishing rod in your hand and a smile on your face. Thanks, Granddad." He touched the headstone with his fingertips.

"Come on, Striker, or you'll be late to your own wedding!" his buddy Justice Wilder called out from the limo parked nearby. "If you are, your future mother-in-law will kill you and you'll be joining your grandfather in this cemetery."

As Striker joined him in the limo, Justice said, "That woman does not like having her schedule messed up. Reminds me of that drill sergeant in boot camp, remember? Sergeant Berg, the Second Hat."

"He's coming to the wedding."

"You're kidding, right?"

Striker just grinned.

He and his best man Justice were both wearing their dress blue uniform as were Striker's brothers and Justice's brother, Sam, when they arrived at the church with one minute to spare. Ben was still on deployment overseas and wasn't able to attend.

"I was just telling your brothers how you caught the bouquet at my wedding," Sam was saying.

"You hotshots better watch out, or I'll have Kate toss her bouquet at one of you," Striker warned his brothers.

"You better watch out, we've decorated your getaway car," his brother Rad replied. He was the practical joker in the family. "By the way, nice bumper sticker you had on there. 'I wasn't born here in Texas but I got here as fast I could.'" Rad slapped him on the back.

"Good luck, son." His dad gave him an unexpected hug. Striker knew that his decision to leave active duty had been hard on his dad. They'd never talked about it, that wasn't their way. But the look his dad gave him said he'd accepted Striker's decision.

Everything was a blur to Striker after that. He did notice that Elizabeth and his mom were waving at each other across the aisle like best friends. Tex was grinning at him. The church was filled with Marines, and with employees from King Oil as well as Kate's friends from Children's Services. Tony was there, too, handing Consuela a tissue to wipe the tears away.

Then his focus was on Kate; on the moment when he first saw her walking down the aisle toward him on her father's arm, looking heart-stoppingly beautiful in her wedding dress. She was wearing the pearl necklace he'd given her. Her blue eyes reflected her love for him.

Her voice was steady as she repeated their vows. So was his. But he felt the tremor in her fingers as he held her hand. He lifted her hand to his lips, to kiss her fingers in a silent reassurance.

"I now pronounce you husband and wife. You may…" Neither one of them waited for the minister to finish before they kissed. The sound of the Dixie Chicks singing "Cowboy Take Me Away" filled the church, accompanied by the crowd of Marines letting out cheers of *oooh-rah!*

"I'm as happy as a short cowboy dancing with a tall cowgirl," Striker murmured against her mouth.

Kate laughed, removing her lips from his, but not far. "You're not dancing with anyone but me. You're not kissing anyone, not loving anyone other than me."

"I wouldn't want to." He adored her with his eyes, seduced her with his voice. "You're the only one for me."

As Striker lowered his lips to hers, Kate was filled with the satisfaction that only comes from knowing that this was where she was meant to be—in the arms of the man she loved.

And still the Dixie Chicks sang, and the Marines shouted, and above it all was the sound of Tex's booming voice. "Now that's what I call a Texas wedding!"

*   *   *   *   *

Watch for Cathie Linz's MEN OF HONOR
series to continue with Ben Kozlowski's story in
CINDERELLA'S SWEET-TALKING MARINE
coming this July only from Silhouette Romance.

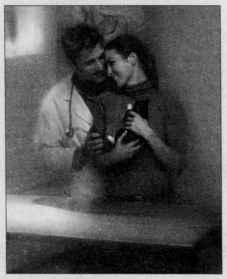

eHARLEQUIN.com

Looking for today's most popular
books at great prices?
At www.eHarlequin.com, we offer:

- An **extensive selection** of romance
  books by top authors!

- **New** releases, Themed Collections
  and hard-to-find **backlist.**

- A sneak peek at Upcoming books.

- Enticing book **excerpts** and **back
  cover copy!**

- Read recommendations from other
  readers (and post your own)!

- Find out what everybody's reading
  in **Bestsellers.**

- **Save BIG** with everyday discounts
  and exclusive online offers!

- Easy, convenient **24-hour shopping.**

- Our **Romance Legend** will help select
  reading that's *exactly* right for you!

**Your purchases are 100%
guaranteed—so shop online
at www.eHarlequin.com today!**

If you enjoyed what you just read,
then we've got an offer you can't resist!

Take 2 bestselling
love stories FREE!

Plus get a FREE surprise gift!

SILHOUETTE *Romance*®

COMING NEXT MONTH

#1722 THE BLACK KNIGHT'S BRIDE—
Myrna Mackenzie
The Brides of Red Rose

Susanna Wright figured a town without men was just the place
for a love-wary single mom to start over, but then she ended up
on former bad boy Brady Malone's doorstep. Despite the fact
that Brady's defenses rivaled a medieval knight's armor, he
agreed to help the delicate damsel in distress. Now she planned
to help this handsome recluse out of his shell—and into her
arms!

#1723 BECAUSE OF BABY—Donna Clayton
Soulmates

Once upon a time there was a sexy widower whose precious
two-year-old daughter simply wouldn't quiet down. Suddenly
a beautiful woman named Fern appeared, but while she calmed
his cranky child, she sent *his* heart racing! Paul Roland knew it
would take something more magical than a pixie-like nanny to
bring romance into his life. But magic didn't exist...did it?

#1724 THE DADDY'S PROMISE—Shirley Jump

Anita Ricardo wanted a family but Mr. Right was nowhere
to be found—enter the Do-It-Yourself Sperm Bank. But
the pregnant self-starter's happily-ever-after wasn't working
out—her house was falling apart, her money was gone and
Luke Dole was turning up everywhere! She agreed to tutor
the handsome widower's rebellious daughter, but *Luke* was
the one teaching her Chemistry 101....

#1725 MAKE ME A MATCH—Alice Sharpe

When Lora Gifford decided to sidetrack her matchmaking
mother and grandmother by hooking them up with loves of
their own, she never counted on infuriating, heart-stopping,
sexy-as-sin veterinarian Jon Woods sidetracking her from her
mission. Plan B: Use kisses, caresses—*any means possible!*—
to get the stubborn vet to make his temporary stay permanent.